The Maze of the Menacing Minotaur

CRISPIN BOYER

Illustrated by Andy Elkerton

UNDER THE *Stars*

NATIONAL GEOGRAPHIC

Since 1888, the National Geographic Society has funded more than 12,000 research, exploration, and preservation projects around the world. The Society receives funds from National Geographic Partners, LLC, funded in part by your purchase. A portion of the proceeds from this book supports this vital work. To learn more, visit natgeo.com/info.

NATIONAL GEOGRAPHIC and Yellow Border Design are trademarks of the National Geographic Society, used under license.

Under the Stars is a trademark of National Geographic Partners, LLC.

For more information, visit nationalgeographic.com, call 1-877-873-6846, or write to the following address:

National Geographic Partners
1145 17th Street N.W.
Washington, D.C. 20036-4688 U.S.A.

Visit us online at nationalgeographic.com/books

For librarians and teachers: nationalgeographic.com/books/librarians-and-educators

More for kids from National Geographic: natgeokids.com

National Geographic Kids magazine inspires children to explore their world with fun yet educational articles on animals, science, nature, and more. Using fresh storytelling and amazing photography, *Nat Geo Kids* shows kids ages 6 to 14 the fascinating truth about the world—and why they should care. **kids.nationalgeographic.com/subscribe**

For rights or permissions inquiries, please contact National Geographic Books Subsidiary Rights: bookrights@natgeo.com

Library of Congress Cataloging-in-Publication Data
Names: Boyer, Crispin, author.
Title: The maze of the menacing minotaur / Crispin Boyer.
Description: Washington : National Geographic Kids, 2020. | Series: Zeus the mighty; 2 | Audience: Ages 8-12. | Audience: Grades 4-6.
Identifiers: LCCN 2019035893 (print) | LCCN 2019035894 (ebook) | ISBN 9781426337567 (hardcover) | ISBN 9781426337574 (library binding) | ISBN 9781426337581 (ebook)
Subjects: CYAC: Pets--Fiction. | Adventure and adventurers--Fiction. | Labyrinths--Fiction. | Mythology, Greek--Fiction. | Pet shops--Fiction.
Classification: LCC PZ7.1.C6947 Maz 2020 (print) | LCC PZ7.1.C6947 (ebook) | DDC [Fic]--dc23
LC record available at https://lccn.loc.gov/2019035893
LC ebook record available at https://lccn.loc.gov/2019035894

Designed by Amanda Larsen
Hand-lettering by Jay Roeder

Printed in U.S.A.
20/WOR/1

For Sue the wise
—C.B.

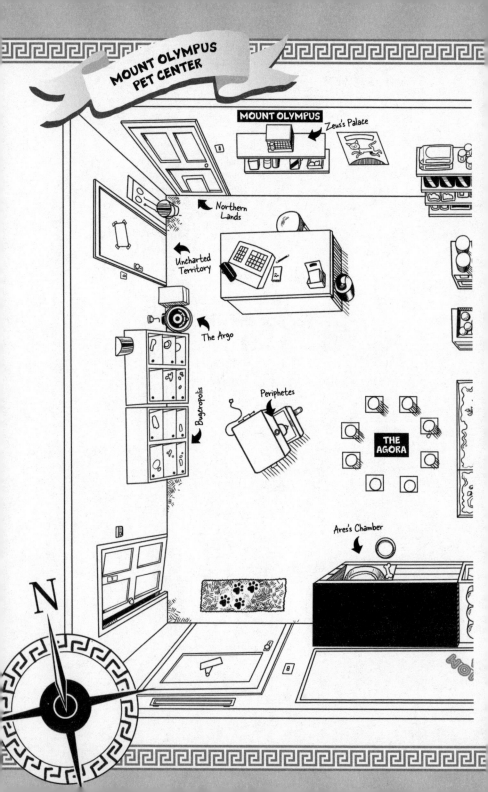

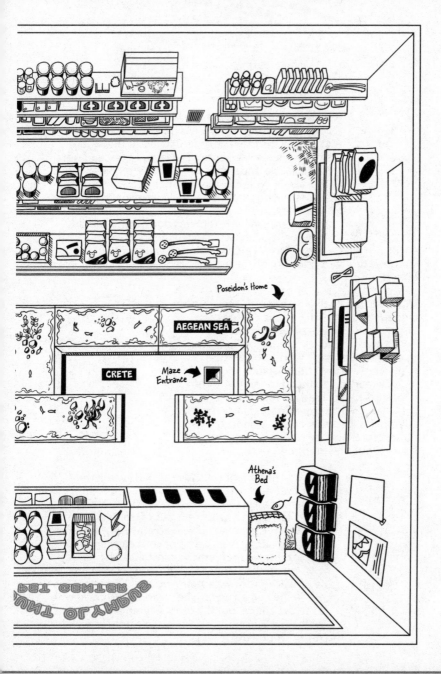

Zeus is a golden hamster with a cloud-shaped patch on his cheek. Zeus believes he's the king of all the other animals that live at the Mount Olympus Pet Center. The favorite rescued pet of Artie, the shop's owner, Zeus genuinely cares about his fellow Olympians but also sees them as minions that should follow him on nightly adventures, which often go awry. When humans aren't around, he scrambles down from "Mount Olympus," the highest shelf in the shop where his enclosure is, and pictures himself wearing a white chiton—a fine shirt people wore in ancient Greece—and a crown-like gilded laurel wreath.

Demeter is a small grasshopper with a big heart. Once a resident of the rescue center's Bugcropolis (the city of insects), she's now Zeus's constant, loyal companion and loves to explore the shop's world. She wears a sash of lettuce over her shoulder and a laurel wreath on her head to represent the Greek goddess of the harvest, for whom she's named. The youngest and fastest of the Olympians, Demeter can fly in short bursts. But don't let her size fool you—this is one courageous grasshopper!

Athena is the wise gray tabby cat that lives in the front window of Mount Olympus Pet Center. Named after the goddess of wisdom, Athena often tries to keep Zeus out of trouble when he starts dreaming up wild adventures. Her quick and clever thinking helps settle arguments and solve problems. For instance, she figured out how to steer the *Argo*, a robot vacuum, which she now captains around the pet center. In the human world, she wears a gold collar with an owl charm, but the other Olympians see her wearing a laurel crown and two thin gold bracelets that wrap around her front paws.

Ares the pug is the strongest of the pet center Olympians. Courageous and impulsive like the god of war, Ares is the first to jump into an adventure and face any monster. But his excitement can sometimes get the better of him. (One time he accidentally sat on Poseidon's hose and almost suffocated the pufferfish!) Ares loves to be called a good boy and can eat an entire handful of Mutt Nuggets in one sitting, which probably contributes to his "meatloaf-ish" body. He wears a spiked collar and, among the Olympians, a bronze Spartan helmet.

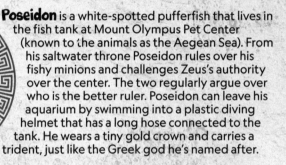

Poseidon is a white-spotted pufferfish that lives in the fish tank at Mount Olympus Pet Center (known to the animals as the Aegean Sea). From his saltwater throne Poseidon rules over his fishy minions and challenges Zeus's authority over the center. The two regularly argue over who is the better ruler. Poseidon can leave his aquarium by swimming into a plastic diving helmet that has a long hose connected to the tank. He wears a tiny gold crown and carries a trident, just like the Greek god he's named after.

Artemis "Artie" Ambrosia is the owner of Mount Olympus Pet Center. In Greek mythology Artemis is the goddess of hunting and wild animals—so it makes sense that Artie has rescued the animals living at the center. It also makes sense that she named all her rescued animals after Greek gods, because she loves Greek mythology. She even listens to *Greeking Out,* a podcast that retells the famous myths and gives the animals crazy ideas for their adventures. Artie plans to open a rescue center next door to Mount Olympus so she can find *fur*-ever homes for more animals.

Phineus is a grizzled old gray hamster that Zeus believes is the blind soothsayer from a Greek myth called "Jason and the Argonauts." Living in the dark, abandoned shop next to the pet center, Phineus meets Zeus after the mighty hamster saves the old critter from a colony of Harpies. (In the human world, they're actually bats!) His long whiskers look like a beard and he uses an old toothpick as a cane. The wise but mysterious Phineus once knew Artie and speaks in riddles. So perhaps there's more to this odd old fellow than meets the eye.

ARTEMIS AMBROSIA DIPPED HER FINGERTIPS into the cool water of the fish tank, startling a pufferfish just below the surface. "Ooh, that's refreshing, Poseidon," she said to the fish. "Mind if I dive in to cool off?"

Poseidon puffed up and raced away. "Just kidding, buddy," Artemis said, giggling. "I wouldn't dare intrude upon your kingdom." She pulled out her fingers and flicked them at a tan pug who sat panting at her feet. He caught the droplets on his tongue and slobbered happily. "You know that's salt water, right, Ares?"

Artemis—Artie for short—stepped away from the fish tanks and checked the thermostat on the wall. Spring had sprung in Athens, Georgia, but a rare cold snap had forced Artie to turn on the furnace. The ancient heating system was working a little too well. She wiped her brow and cranked the temperature down, then resumed her evening routine closing up Mount Olympus Pet Center while Ares shuffled along at her heels. She dusted off a display of hamster mazes, arranged a rack of ball chuckers, then shut down the cash register. She stopped by the kennels and secured the pug in his crate. "That's a good god of war."

Artie turned to look up at the tallest shelf in the store, high above the cash register, where a familiar golden hamster watched her from his cage. "Keeping cool up there, Zeus?" She walked to the shelf and stood on her tippy-toes to peek in. Zeus had backed away from the bars of his home and plopped into the new bed cut from a golden-colored fleece material. Artie stuck a finger through the bars to scratch a patch of white fur on the hamster's cheek. "Nighty night, Zeus the Mighty. Don't even think about busting out for a midnight dip!"

The hamster gave a squeak and Artie shook her head. It had been a week since she caught him hamster-paddling in Poseidon's aquarium, and she still couldn't get over it.

Artie zipped up her jacket and switched off the lights, plunging the center into the dim red glow of the Mount Olympus Pet Center sign. As she opened the front door, Artie turned to the hamster on his shelf. "And don't you sneak out again. I'd hate to lose you!"

〰

CHAPTER 1

ZEUS THE MIGHTY WAS NOT LOST. HE'D been wandering in a warren of metal passages for the past hour. He was deep underground, a long way from his palace on Mount Olympus, where he ruled over the other Greek gods. He wasn't even sure if he was still in Greece. But Zeus was definitely, absolutely, not lost.

"Are we lost?" asked Demeter, Zeus's most frequent Olympian companion. "This maze is just so … so …"

"Mazelike?" Zeus finished her thought. "And no, we're not lost—I don't get lost." He rubbed his chin as he inspected yet another fork in the tunnel. The two passages ahead appeared no different than every tunnel behind them: halls with metal walls lit by a distant orange glow.

"Sure, why would you get lost?" replied Demeter. The goddess of harvests nibbled nervously from the lettuce sash she wore across her shoulder. "I mean, mazes are, like, a hamster thing."

"This isn't a hamster thing, pal," Zeus said. "I don't get lost because I'm Zeus, the king of the gods. Always knowing where to go comes with the job."

"True." Demeter nodded. "You always know where to go. Most of the time … Sometimes…" She looked at the fork in the tunnel. "So … where do we go?"

Zeus sniffed at one of the tunnels, then shrugged. "This-a-way." He picked a direction and wandered onward, his gilded laurel-wreath crown and the golden thunderbolt emblem on his shoulder gleaming faintly in the dim orange light.

Demeter watched him fade into the gloom. An odd shiver ran up her back, and she had the sudden urge to check behind her. "Someone there?" she asked, glancing over her shoulder. But she was alone. Shuddering, Demeter quickly caught up with Zeus on her powerful grasshopper legs.

The two Olympians had come across the entrance to

this underground maze earlier that night while exploring Crete, an area of land surrounded on three sides by the Aegean Sea. Here they had nearly stumbled into a rectangular pit, more than big enough to fit the hamster and his companion. Zeus had paid little mind to this pit during past excursions to Crete; it had always been blocked by a metal grate. Tonight, the grate was gone—just one of the many strange changes happening in Greece ever since Artie's friend Callie had arrived to meddle with the landscape.

Zeus had wondered if this pit led to a shortcut across Greece, or to a new underworld realm, or maybe to the secret lair of Phineus, the mysterious soothsayer who had helped Zeus on a previous adventure. If nothing else, Zeus thought, going underground might give them an escape from the heat wave that gripped Greece.

So they had entered. But this maze offered no relief from the blistering temperatures. In fact, the deeper they delved, the hotter it got. The normally spiky fur on Zeus's head flopped over his crown. Soon he was overheating beneath the white fabric of his royal chiton, even though, like all Olympian attire, it felt like it was barely there.

"I swear we've walked under every part of Greece," Demeter muttered, her antennae sagging. "It's a good thing we're not lost or I'd be worried—"

"What in blazes is that?" Zeus interrupted as they rounded a corner. The two had reached the entrance to a much larger cavern. Heat crashed over them like a tsunami. The air shimmered with it. Out of the gloom loomed a terrifying sight: a towering monstrous beast with ash-covered horns. It fixed them with beady eyes set above fiery orange nostrils linked by a silver chain.

"You see that big bull ... thing standing there, too, don't you, Zeus?" Demeter asked flatly. "Or is this heat playing tricks on my eyes?"

Zeus's head was swimming. He shook it and tried to focus on the monster's eyes, its nostrils, that chain. Then he saw its mouth, locked in a grimace of square teeth shut tight.

"I see it," Zeus whispered. "Do you see what I see poking from its teeth?"

"That's not ..." Demeter answered slowly. "That's not fur, is it?"

"I think we should go," Zeus said. He turned and searched for the tunnel they had come from but saw dozens of openings all around the cavern. "Blast it, which one's the way out?" Zeus dared not look back at the horned beast in the center of the cavern. He could practically feel the monster bearing down on them. He couldn't think clearly. Both Zeus and Demeter felt like they were moments away from melting.

Just as he was about to collapse, a pair of what felt like furry posts tapped Zeus on his shoulder.

He whirled to see a brown spider as tall as he was standing behind them, its eight legs covered with prickly hairs. The spider fixed them both with two large dark eyes set above four smaller ones. A tiara encrusted with red stones sat atop the spider's head.

"Now I'm definitely seeing stuff," Demeter muttered.

The spider stared at Zeus and said in a raspy voice, "Greetings, two-eyes. Are you here to defeat the heat?"

Zeus blinked. "Well, uh, of course I could do that," he stammered, "but, honestly, I'm just feeling kind of bleh right now. You ever have one of those days?"

The spider stared at Zeus with her dark eyes.

"Anyway," Zeus pressed on, "I'd rather not do a job at all than do it badly, you know?"

"Then you need to skitter out of this place," the spider said.

"Skitter where?" Zeus said. "We're lost."

"You said you don't get lost!" Demeter yelled.

"Take this." The spider raised a fuzzy leg holding the end of a long strand of web. "Follow it. It will lead you from the beast, away from the heat, to where you began tonight's journey."

Zeus saw that the web thread stretched into one of the tunnels along the cavern's edge—and suddenly recognized it as the tunnel from which they had entered. "Wait, how'd you get that thread behind us?" Zeus looked from the tunnel to the spider and back again. "Have you been following us?"

"I knew I sensed someone behind us!" Demeter said.

"What, like some sort of spider sense?" Zeus asked weakly. He was a bit wobbly on his feet.

Demeter ignored his comment and eyed the spider. "I don't know if I trust her. I mean, grasshoppers and spiders don't typically get along."

The spider returned her gaze coldly.

"I trust her more than the fire-breathing bull

monster." Zeus took the thread and wrapped its end round his paw.

The two Olympians followed the thread to the tunnel, where Zeus stopped and turned back to the spider. She'd remained in the cavern.

"Thanks, um … " Zeus said, prompting for her name.

"Ariadne," the spider replied.

"Air-ee-add-nee," Zeus repeated, careful to get the name just right. "I'm Zeus, but I'm sure you already knew that. I'm a pretty big deal."

"I know who you are." Ariadne's dark eyes glittered more brightly than the rubies in her tiara.

The webbing tugged Zeus's paw as Demeter hopped ahead. "Okay, then. I'll be back to beat this heat."

Ariadne stared but said nothing.

"I just need to rest up," Zeus continued awkwardly, "get back on top of my game. Maybe bring a few friends." The thread tugged again. "Okay, gotta go." Zeus turned and followed Demeter out of the cavern as quickly as his unsteady legs could carry him, eager to escape the horned monster that had nearly melted them on the spot.

CHAPTER 2

THENA, GODDESS OF WISDOM, SAT TALL at the helm of the *Argo*, her gray mane ruffling in the hot breeze as she held a steady course across the Aegean Sea's southern coastline. At the bow sat Poseidon, lord of the sea, floating in his dive helmet. Ares, the god of war, trotted on foot behind the *Argo*.

"You have the sharpest eyes out of all of us, Poseidon," Athena said to her fellow Olympian. "Any sign of them?"

"Neither hide nor hair," replied the pufferfish. He pressed his face against the clear wall of his helmet and held his fins like binoculars in front of his oversize eyes.

"I don't see any hides or hairs neither." Ares peered this way and that as he walked. "Wait, does Demeter even have hides and hairs?"

Poseidon swiveled to see the pug with his bronze Spartan war helmet low over his face, its plume of brushy black fur sprouting from the top. Only Ares's slobbery tongue was visible between the cheek guards.

"Honestly, war god," Poseidon said, gesturing with his trident, "I don't know how you breathe with that bucket on your head, let alone see anything."

"Bucket?" Ares barked. "You're the guy with a helmet full of water."

"You are aware this is more than just a fashion accessory?" Poseidon tapped his helmet. It was the key to his traveling in the realm of air-breathing animals. The helmet received a supply of oxygen-rich water through a hose that stretched all the way to the Aegean Sea.

"You're lucky you get to travel in your own swimming pool," Athena said, panting from the heat.

"My aching pectoral fins don't feel so lucky," Poseidon said, flexing the fins on each side. "I'd much rather be puffed out at home than cooped up in this thing, bumbling all over Greece looking for our foolhardy king."

"I bet Zeus and Demeter are on some supercool adventure without us," Ares said. "I hate missing out."

"I hope he hasn't gotten in over his head," Athena said.

"More than likely they're off on a wild-goose chase," said Poseidon, "perhaps hunting after that imaginary chum of Zeus's again. Phinangle or some such."

"Phineus," Athena corrected, "the soothsayer. And that thought has crossed my mind. Zeus is determined to prove that old hamster is real."

"Well, if he is real," said Poseidon, "then I'll eat my trident—"

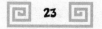

"STOP!" hollered a figure that suddenly appeared in front of the *Argo*.

"Hold fast!" Athena slapped the silver button and brought the *Argo* to a jarring halt. Poseidon's dive helmet rolled off the bow of the vessel, bouncing several times and sending the pufferfish somersaulting inside. Ares, caught in mid-trot, bowled over the *Argo*, knocking Athena overboard. She landed nimbly and silently except for the clink-clink of her golden owl-shaped charm.

"What was that?!" Ares shouted, trying to look everywhere at once.

"More of a who than a what," Athena answered.

"It's me—Zeus!" said the golden hamster standing tall before the *Argo*. His royal robes gleamed and fell just right as always. Beside him stood Demeter, her antennae drooping over the gold laurel wreath on her head.

"You trying to get run over?" Athena straightened

her own gilded wreath crown. "Why'd you leap out at us like that?"

"How else am I supposed to stop you?" Zeus asked.

"Well, we're stopped." Poseidon pumped his fins to right himself in the churning water of his helmet.

"Where'd you guys come from?" Ares asked.

"Over there!" Zeus jabbed a paw at the gap in the dunes that marked the entrance to Crete. "There's something you need to see on Crete!"

"What kind of thing?" Ares sniffed at the entrance.

"Well, for starters, there's a pit in the ground," Demeter said, "and it leads to a really hot maze. And a monster with flaming nostrils and big horns! And a huuuge scary spider … who actually turned out to be pretty nice. We'd be melted into puddles down there if she hadn't helped us find our way out!"

"The monster is causing this heat wave!" Zeus turned to reenter Crete. "I'm sure we could deal with it together. Everyone follow me to the maze entrance!!"

"Wait—now?" Demeter said weakly. "I'm still kind of woozy."

"Not now," Athena said. "Something's wrong with our ride. It won't start!" She had been pawing frantically at the start button but the *Argo*'s motor didn't hum back to life.

"Maybe it just needs a kick," Demeter said, thumping the vessel's hull with her hind legs.

"Maybe it just needs a lick," Ares said, slobbering over the *Argo*'s rubbery deck.

"I don't think it needs either of those things," said Athena as she inspected the machine's various crystals. They no longer glowed with their normal light.

"Well, isn't this just wonderful?" Poseidon whirled in his helmet to stare at Zeus. "We wasted our night searching for Zeus and he broke the *Argo*."

"Broke the *Argo*?" Zeus repeated. "I didn't even touch the *Argo*!"

"The *Argo* worked," Poseidon said. "You showed up. The *Argo* doesn't work. Ergo, you broke the *Argo*."

"Oh, you go *Argo* the ergo or whatever, puff-'n'-stuff!" Zeus snapped.

Athena stepped between Zeus and Poseidon and held up a braceleted paw. "Olympians, this is getting us nowhere fast. We can't just squabble here in the open all night. Let's abandon ship and figure this out later. Sun's coming up!"

"She's right," Demeter said, seeing the first rays creep across the plains of Greece. "Artie will be here any minute!"

"Aww, but I wanna go see the bull monster!" Ares said, trotting toward the entrance of Crete.

"Uh-uh! Get back here, war god!" Athena commanded. "We'll deal with that later."

Ares tucked his tail and moped, whimpering softly.

"Fine," Zeus agreed reluctantly. "I guess we should rest up and strategize and whatnot."

"And I do have my own kingdom to rule." Poseidon rolled his helmet toward the Aegean Sea, where his minions were waiting to hoist him up by his lifeline and back into the water. Athena and Ares ran home across the plains of Greece. Zeus and Demeter scrambled toward Mount Olympus. Everyone wanted to get back before Artie arrived to begin her day. For now, the monster in the maze—and the horrible heat wave it created—would have to wait.

CHAPTER 3

ZEUS CLAMBERED UP TO HIS PALACE JUST in time to see a flash of red hair as Artie entered the main portal to ancient Greece. She was followed by a wiry woman with short sandy hair carrying her usual bulging bag.

"Artie brought Callie again," said Demeter, already lounging against the pillars of the palace, snacking on her sash of lettuce.

"Of course she did." Zeus sighed loudly as he joined Demeter at the pillars. "Callie being here is like the new normal." Below them, Artie peeled off her jacket and checked the thermostat. "Huh, I turned this thing down last night, but it's still pretty toasty in here," she said to Callie. "You mind checking the furnace today?"

"I'll add it to the list," Callie said.

"List?" Zeus threw up his paws. "Now Callie has a whole list of stuff to do?"

"Yep, sounds like she won't stop hanging out with Artie anytime soon." Demeter said.

Zeus—and all the Olympians—loved Artie. She looked after all the inhabitants of land, sea, and air, cleaning their living quarters, making sure the food was fresh and tasty, and dealing with the other humans who frequently paid a visit to Greece. Best of all, the pockets of her jeans were always stuffed with treats of every sort.

Callie was a different story. Since she arrived, she'd been a constant thorn in Zeus's side. Each day she brought some fantastic new artifact or frightening beast, which she dragged into uncharted territory before Zeus had a chance to investigate. Who knew what Callie was up to in that mysterious realm, which was hidden behind a portal to the west? Artie said Callie was expanding Greece. All Zeus ever saw her do was break things and make a mess.

"Why's the robot vacuum on the loose?" Callie asked Artie. Zeus watched Callie examine the *Argo*. "Battery's dead," she said. "Maybe your kitty took it for another

joyride." Callie turned and
glared at Athena, who
was innocently licking a
paw in her bed near the
kennels.

"After last week's
insanity, that would
almost seem normal,"
Artie said, laughing.

Callie placed the
Argo into its dock near the
portal to uncharted territory. "Okay, I'm off to work." She
walked through the portal, leaving Artie to her caretaking
duties.

On Mount Olympus, Zeus relaxed. He always felt
better when Callie was out of Greece. She distracted him
from one of his most important duties: planning the
Olympians' adventures. And right now, the quest at hand
was particularly urgent. Whatever monster lived down in
that maze was clearly responsible for the heat wave. If
they didn't deal with it soon, the heat might bake everyone
in Greece.

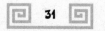

Zeus looked out from Mount Olympus. All his fellow Olympians were settled into their usual places. Ares was scarfing down Mutt Nuggets in his chambers to the south, with Athena preening nearby. Poseidon glided beneath the waves of the Aegean Sea. His minions had stowed his dive helmet in its usual spot on the sea's gravel bottom. Artie, meanwhile, was going about her daily routine, oblivious to the horned, heat-breathing threat lurking beneath her feet. She heaped salad into a bowl for Kiko, a vegetarian dragon whose lair sat high in the northern hills, then doted over the leggy inhabitants of the Bugcropolis, in between helping the random humans who entered Greece through its main portal. She provided them with various relics or snacks or supplies, then sent them on their way. These humans always left after a quick visit—unlike Callie.

Afternoon shadows were creeping across the countryside when familiar harp music began playing from below. Both Zeus and Demeter saw Artie fiddling with the black device she carried with her everywhere. She tapped her finger on the sleek rectangle and the harp music got louder. Then it faded as a woman's voice began speaking: "Welcome to Greeking Out, your weekly podcast that delivers the goods on Greek gods and epic tales of triumphant heroes. I'm your host, the Oracle of Wi-Fi."

"Good," Zeus said. "Maybe now we can get some answers!"

"This time," the Oracle continued, "brace yourselves for the most terrifying tale in Greek mythology—the tale of the Minotaur."

"The minute tour?" Zeus repeated carefully.

"How terrifying could a minute-long tour be?" Demeter asked.

"Oooooh, this sounds like a scary one," Artie said as she began dusting the Bugcropolis.

CHAPTER 4

THE ORACLE OF WI-FI WAS A REAL know-it-all, an endless source of wisdom. She wasn't so much a teacher; her tales could be confusing. She was more like a fortune-teller, offering hints about the next big adventure. Whenever Artie summoned *Greeking Out* on her device, the Olympians listened carefully.

"This is the story of a legendary hero, a brilliant princess, a mad inventor, and a terrifying monster that lurked in the center of a maze," the Oracle said.

"A terrifying monster?" Demeter whispered.

"In a maze?" added Zeus.

"Now sit back and heed the Oracle's words, listeners, as I breathe new life into one of the earliest stories ever written. A glimpse of how the ancient Greeks saw their world. A tale told and retold for three thousand years."

Zeus rolled his eyes and mouthed along to the Oracle's words, the same speech she gave at the start of all her tales.

"This episode of *Greeking Out* is brought to you by Fuzzy Feast. Tasty treats for growing rodents, Fuzzy Feast packs the vitamins that hamsters crave!"

"I know what Fuzzy Feast is, Oracle—I eat it every day," Zeus groused. "Now get to the good stuff!"

The Oracle obliged: "Our story begins with Theseus, prince of the great city of Athens. His father the king wouldn't accept Theseus as his heir unless the young man could prove himself. As a test, the king hid a powerful relic beneath a monstrous slab in the countryside to see if his son was clever and strong enough to find it."

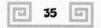

"Ooh," Zeus whispered, "powerful relics are my favorite relics."

"Young Theseus was strong, fearless, and wise—the ultimate Greek hero. It's no wonder some suspected he was actually the son of Poseidon."

Demeter nearly choked on her lettuce sash. "Son of Poseidon?!"

"Nah, that can't be right." Zeus shook his head. "I think the Oracle is just being extra Oracle-y. Let's see where she goes with this."

"Barely a day went by that young Theseus didn't accomplish some heroic deed. He walloped bandits and bullies. He found the relic his father had hidden: a legendary spear. The people of Athens loved this dashing young man who took each challenge by the horns—which made him the right hero to tackle a terrifying new threat lurking beneath ancient Greece. It was a creature with the body of a human and the head of a bull: the Minotaur."

"Minotaur," Zeus repeated, clapping his paws. "Not 'minute tour.' That's the monster we saw this morning."

"I bet he got that name because he tore some hero apart in a minute," Demeter said. "Here's hoping the

Oracle tells us how to beat this Minotaur."

"The Minotaur lived at the center of a maze deep beneath Crete," the lesson continued. "Anyone who entered was doomed to wander its twisting corridors, slowly making their way to the center. The closer they got, the hotter the air became, like they were walking in an oven, until finally they were roasted inside and out, a well-done meal for the Minotaur at the maze's scalding heart."

Zeus remembered the animal fur stuck in the Minotaur's teeth and shuddered.

The Oracle continued. "Theseus resolved to rid the land of the Minotaur menace. He delved into the maze beneath Crete—"

"Artie, you mind coming next door?" called Callie, who had emerged from whatever she was doing in uncharted territory. "I need to know where you want the hair cleanout for the doggy-bath station."

"Sure thing," Artie said.

"Shush!" Zeus exclaimed. "I can't hear what the Oracle's saying."

Nor would he. Artie paused *Greeking Out* and followed Callie into uncharted territory.

CHAPTER 5

"**W**HAT'S A HAIR CLEANOUT?" DEMETER asked in the silence.

"Obviously a hair cleanout is an incredibly important thing," Zeus replied calmly, the white patch of fur on his cheek twitching, "certainly more important than learning about legendary spears or impossible mazes." His voice grew louder with each word. "Or how to rid Greece of a heat-breathing, bull-horned, hero-munching MONSTER!" Zeus hopped onto his exercise wheel and began running at full speed.

Demeter stood by quietly and let him sprint out his frustration. Zeus ran out of steam and plopped down on his backside, panting hard.

"How come every time we're about to get to the good

part of *Greeking Out*, Callie comes in and opens her yap? Who interrupts the Oracle? I mean, who does that?!"

"Maybe we don't need to hear the Oracle's tale to figure out how to defeat the Minotaur," said Demeter, hoping to calm Zeus's jangled nerves. "We have someone better than the Oracle!"

"We do?" Zeus asked. Then, after thinking for a moment, "We do! Phineus!"

"No, no, I meant that spider—"

"Where's my god of war?!" Callie squealed. She had already returned from uncharted territory along with Artie, who walked to the Aegean Sea and began sprinkling flakes of food onto its waves.

Down on the plains of Greece, Ares dashed to Callie and rolled over at her feet as she scratched behind his ear. "Who's a good boy?" Callie cooed.

"Ares sure is chummy with Callie," Demeter said, watching from the palace's pillars.

"Ares would be chummy with Medusa if she gave him Mutt Nuggets." Zeus shuffled over to mope next to Demeter. "We can't stop the Minotaur until Artie and Callie scram for the night." He saw that Callie had stopped fawning over Ares and was now piecing together some mysterious new artifact near the portal to uncharted territory. Whatever it was, it was huge—a featureless slab as tall as Greece's rugged hills.

"What's that contraption?" Demeter asked Zeus.

"What's that contraption?" Artie asked Callie at nearly the same time.

"It's a drill press," Callie replied.

"Cool … What's a drill press?" Artie said.

"It's a big thing that puts holes in smaller things. I'll need it tomorrow to build shelves, so I wanted to get it ready tonight." Callie wiped a forearm across her forehead.

"Oh, shoot," Artie said. "We forgot to check the furnace today!"

"Want me to check it now?" Callie grabbed her tool bag.

Artie glanced at her rectangular artifact. "Whoa, it's late. We'll do it tomorrow. Let me just crack a window real quick." She grabbed her coat and keys and headed to the main portal to Greece, where she cranked open a glass panel above the entrance. She turned and addressed the

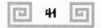

animals. "Nighty night, Olympians. Stay cool—and out of trouble!"

Artie switched off the light, and the two humans departed Greece.

"About time!" Zeus exclaimed, then shouted across Greece: "Olympians, assemble! Usual spot!" He turned to Demeter. "Head on down and get everyone up to speed, will ya?"

"You got it." Demeter squeezed through the pillars of the palace and flexed her tiny wings, which allowed her to glide great distances and make soft landings from frightening heights, even the tallest peak in the land. She leapt toward the distant Olympians.

Zeus paused only long enough to grab the aegis shield from its spot on the wall and attach it to his arm. The silver box-shaped shield was one of his prized relics. Inside was an enchanted ribbon that Zeus could use to pull himself to distant objects, sort of like a grappling hook. Equipped for adventure, Zeus slipped through the back door of his palace and slid down the long rope that connected the summit of Mount Olympus to the floor of Greece. He hit the ground running toward the meeting spot.

The Olympians always assembled at the Agora. It was an open area in the heart of Greece surrounded by eight columns, each coiled in coarse rope. Zeus arrived panting hard and feeling like he was about to topple over in the heat. All the other Olympians were there except for Poseidon, who rolled up in his diving helmet, his lifeline trailing back to the Aegean Sea.

Before Zeus could catch his breath, Athena announced, "We need to stop the Minotaur."

Zeus looked up in surprise. "Right … exactly, Athena. So Demeter told you that the Minotaur and the monster we saw in the maze are one and the same?"

"I'd already figured that out from the Oracle of Wi-Fi," Athena said.

"We get to play with a bull monster?!" Ares spun in place, a blur of tan fur. His helmet teetered above his wrinkly face. "What's the plan, boss?"

"Phineus will know how to stop the Minotaur," Zeus said. "Demeter and I agreed we need to find him first."

"That's … that's not what we …" Demeter trailed off. "Oh, never mind."

"Haven't we wasted enough time searching for this Phineus fellow?" Poseidon asked, puffing up.

"Wasted time, my fuzzy behind!" Zeus's cheek twitched.

Athena stepped between the hamster and pufferfish. "Stop bickering. Maybe instead of falling back into old habits, you two should try working together."

"Fantastic idea, Athena!" Zeus said triumphantly. "Poseidon and I will find Phineus while you all check out the scene on Crete."

"Seriously?" Poseidon deflated.

"Okay, I'll go dig up the Minotaur!" Ares bolted in the direction of the Aegean Sea and the patch of land at its center.

Athena noted Ares's dwindling backside and sighed. "I should really catch up with him. The war god doesn't do well unsupervised."

"What about me, Zeus?" Demeter asked.

"You head back up to Mount Olympus and keep an eye on things."

"Okay. Can I sit on the Fleece?"

"Sure, whatever, just try not to get lettuce bits all over it."

"Yes!" Demeter pumped four legs at once.

"Let's all meet back here in three hours," Athena suggested.

"If we don't find Phineus, do I get that time back?" snapped Poseidon.

Zeus ignored him. He had no doubt they would find the soothsayer. He couldn't wait to show the smug old pufferfish that Phineus was real.

CHAPTER 6

"**W**HERE ARE WE GOING?" POSEIDON ASKED as he rushed to keep up with Zeus.

"Where do you think we're going?" Zeus said coldly. "I mean, it should be pretty obvious."

The two were trekking west from the Agora.

"Obvious, huh?" Poseidon said, tapping his trident against his crown as if deep in thought. "Hmm, if I were a figment of Zeus's imagination, where would I be?"

"Oh, knock it off!" Zeus snapped. "We're going to uncharted territory. That's where I ran into Phineus, remember?"

"I remember he went poof before anyone else could see him," Poseidon said.

Zeus stopped and whirled on Poseidon, who nearly

rolled into him. "What's your beef with me today, fish? I mean, other than the usual bad attitude?"

"Maybe I'm just tired of you treating me like an underling. I mean, you never question Athena's advice. You always call on Ares when you need some muscle. You and Demeter are practically inseparable."

Zeus's expression softened, and his eyes widened in surprise. "Poseidon, are you saying you're jealous?"

"Not at all." Poseidon huffed. "It's just that I'm an Olympian, too, you know. I'm wise. I'm courageous. I'm a king of my own realm, for goodness' sake." Poseidon brandished his trident, the symbol of his authority over the sea. "I'm a formidable fish! I should call the shots once in a while."

Zeus considered Poseidon's words. "I suppose this is my fault," he said at last.

"What?" Poseidon lowered his trident.

"I've made being king of the gods seem too easy," Zeus continued. "Protecting Greece, planning our nightly adventures ... Now everyone thinks they can do it."

"Oh, please." Poseidon crossed his fins.

"I suppose my biggest fault is I'm too brave. Everyone around me can't help but feel inspired."

"Uh-huh. So are you going to let me call the shots or not?"

Zeus shrugged. "Sure." He started walking again. Poseidon, bracing for an argument, drifted idly before following in Zeus's wake, still in shock.

Soon the duo came upon the towering piece of mysterious machinery that Callie had assembled before she left. It looked to them like a featureless four-sided slab of metal reaching well into the sky. Zeus put his paw on its flat metal surface. It felt warm, but then, so did everything in this heat. He could feel something else inside— something humming. "It almost feels … alive," Zeus said.

Poseidon pressed his flat face against his dive helmet and took in the slab from bottom to top. "Certainly there's more to this … whatever it is … than meets the eye. We should examine the other side."

"You're the boss," Zeus said.

The two slowly made their way around the slab. Zeus tilted his head back to observe its smooth surface as they walked. "This thing's kind of—oof!"

He stumbled over what appeared to be a bench protruding from the slab as he rounded a corner. "Ow! This seems like a weird place to put a seat." He got up and ran his paws along the object. It was covered with a rough rubber, which Zeus began prodding.

Poseidon watched Zeus with concern. "Perhaps you shouldn't be messing with that."

"I dunno, feels comfy. Good spot to cool my heels while you decide our next move." Zeus plopped down on the

bench, and the seat sank slightly beneath his weight. *CLICK. VRRRRRRR!* A shrill metallic whine—like metal wheels spinning at high speed—pierced the morning quiet.

"What on earth did you do, Zeus?!" Poseidon shrieked, pressing his fins to his head and sinking to the bottom of his mobile habitat.

"Nothing! I didn't do anything!" Zeus leapt up from the bench, but the noise continued. "Where's that blasted racket coming from?!"

The shrillness deepened into a series of grating sounds, like gears grinding. Zeus and Poseidon stared at each other, not quite believing what they were hearing. The noises had a familiar pattern. They almost sounded like … words.

But then the grating stopped, and the sound resumed its original shrill pitch.

"What did we just hear?" Zeus asked Poseidon.

Before he could answer, the high-pitched whirring deepened into grinding sounds again. This time the words they formed were unmistakable: "YOU JUST HEARD ME!"

"GAAHHH!" both Olympians screamed. Zeus dove

behind Poseidon, who at the same time rolled forward and left Zeus cowering in the open.

The whine deepened into more grinding sounds: "GAZE UPON ME IN WONDER AND FEAR!"

Zeus and Poseidon composed themselves and looked around to find the source of this peculiar voice. A few feet above them, a large open space had been carved into the side of the slab facing them. Within it they saw a massive arm, clad in black metal armor, suspended from the space's ceiling. The arm held a shiny spear forged from golden metal. As the Olympians watched, the arm swung the spear in a wide arc, cutting through the air with a whistling sound, before returning to its original position and becoming still.

"What is that thing?" Zeus asked Poseidon.

"I AM THAT THING," the voice ground out. Zeus and Poseidon looked above the spear-wielding arm and spotted a massive, glowing green eye staring down at them from higher up the slab.

"Who are you?" Zeus shouted in a deep voice, trying to sound intimidating. (And not succeeding, thought Poseidon.)

"I AM PERIPHETES," replied the grating voice. The black arm swung the spear in a flourish, and both Zeus and Poseidon ducked instinctively even though they were below its reach.

Zeus stood up and asked, "And how can we help you today, Peri-Peri-whatever-your-name-is?"

"PERIPHETES!"

Zeus and Poseidon were becoming accustomed to Periphetes' strange way of communicating.

"Right, Pair-a-feeties," Zeus repeated, pronouncing the name carefully. "What do you want?"

"COME CLOSER SO I CAN SHOW YOU MY WEAPON." The arm swung the spear against the side of the slab, making a terrible clang, then swung it again, and again. Zeus could feel the ground vibrating beneath his feet. He noticed that the water was rippling in Poseidon's helmet with each impact.

"We can see your weapon just fine from down here!" Poseidon shouted.

"I wouldn't mind getting a closer look," Zeus muttered.

"Closer look? You get any closer and he'll stick that thing through your thick head."

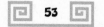

"The thought crossed my mind." Zeus addressed the glowering eyeball, "Hey, if I come up there and check out your spear, are you going to stick it through my head?"

"THROUGH YOUR HEAD? NO. THROUGH YOUR CHEST? YES." Periphetes thrust the spear through the air to punctuate his point.

"Okay, thanks for clarifying." Zeus turned to Poseidon and shrugged. "At least he's honest." He limbered up his shoulders and hefted the aegis shield on his arm.

Poseidon gaped. "You're not actually going up there, are you?"

"The Oracle said that Theseus's father hid a legendary spear beneath a slab in the countryside." Zeus pointed at Periphetes. "That's a slab, and there's our spear. I bet it would make short work of the Minotaur."

"How are you going to get the spear without, you know, getting it jammed through your chest?"

"I'll figure something out," Zeus said. "It's what I do."

Periphetes's metal arm was back to swinging the spear against his metal body. *CLANG! CLANG!*

"EITHER YOU COME UP HERE OR I'M COMING DOWN THERE. ONE WAY OR THE OTHER, I AM

SHOWING YOU MY SPEAR, RODENT!"

"Rodent?!" Zeus shouted angrily, the white patch on his cheek quivering like mad. "That's King Rodent to you, Pair-a-feeties!"

Periphetes shook the spear in anger. His green eye flickered to red, and the entire slab began to vibrate.

"That can't be good," Poseidon muttered, backing his helmet up slowly.

Zeus meanwhile had slid his aegis shield off his arm and set the boxy relic on the ground. The corner of the shield had a small metal tab. Zeus pulled on it, revealing a rigid metal ribbon

that unspooled from the box. The ribbon was inscribed with skinny lines and large numbers. Using both paws, Zeus continued pulling, guiding the ribbon until its metal tab was nearly level with the slab above him. Finally, *click.* The tab hooked on the ledge beneath Periphetes's metal arm. Now all Zeus needed to do was hit the retract button on his shield and he could ride it up to inspect the spear.

"I just want to go on the record as saying that this is an exceedingly foolish move," Poseidon said.

"Your fish minion speaks the truth," came a voice behind them.

Zeus and Poseidon turned to see a frail hamster clad in rags and leaning on a gnarled cane.

"Phineus!" Zeus exclaimed.

"Phineus?" Poseidon said, shock in his voice.

"WHO?!" Periphetes asked.

"HA!" Zeus rounded on Poseidon. "Told you he was real!"

CHAPTER 7

PHINEUS THE SOOTHSAYER WAS EXACTLY as Zeus had remembered him: Gray fur from head to toe. His whiskers hung nearly to his waist like a beard. The only difference was Phineus's figure. He didn't appear quite as frail beneath his rags.

"You seem like you're eating better," Zeus said.

"I'm eating *something*." Phineus patted his meager belly. "Something's better than nothing."

"I saved Phineus from some flying monsters who were swiping all his food," Zeus reminded Poseidon, who was still stunned by the soothsayer's sudden appearance.

"Those Snatchers have flown the coop for good," Phineus said, "thanks to you, lad."

Zeus beamed.

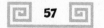

"Okay, hold on," Poseidon said, puffing up slightly in his helmet. "Let's start over. So you're Phineus."

The old hamster smirked.

"The soothsayer who told Zeus how to find the Golden Fleece?"

"I suppose I had something to do with that." Phineus looked the pufferfish up and down. "And you're Poseidon."

Poseidon was taken aback. "How'd you know?"

Phineus poked a thumb at his chest. "Soothsayer."

Zeus chuckled.

"Where have you been?" asked Poseidon.

"Beg your pardon?" Phineus said.

"Where'd you disappear to?" Poseidon pressed on. "Zeus told us you vanished before any of us Olympians could meet you. Where'd you go?"

"Soothsayer business," Phineus said.

"Who cares, Poseidon?" Zeus said. "He's here now. He can give us all kinds of helpful soothsaying!"

"The whole sooth and nothing but the sooth," Phineus agreed.

CLANG! CLANG! Above them, Periphetes had gone back to swinging his spear. The high-pitched whirring deepened to form the words: "ENOUGH TALK DOWN THERE! FACE ME, RODENT! I WANT TO SHOW YOU MY SPEAR!"

"Which rodent?" Phineus yelled up at Periphetes. "Maybe you haven't noticed, but there are two of us now." He nodded at Zeus and smiled. "Ho-ho. Not much for brain power, this Periphetes fella."

"I'm not sure he even has a brain," Zeus said. "I figure it should be easy enough to get the spear from him." He hefted his aegis shield, which was ready to carry Zeus up as soon as he hit the retract button.

Phineus held the tip of his cane over the button. "Zeus, lad, the king of the gods shouldn't be dirtying his paws battling monsters just to collect these knickknacks."

"You have a better idea?" Zeus asked.

"Watch and learn." Before Zeus could say a word, Phineus focused on the glowing eye and yelled, "Say, Periphetes, that is a nice-looking spear."

The compliment seemed to catch Periphetes off guard. The high-pitched whirring held for a long moment until finally it deepened into Periphetes's grating voice: "YES. YES, IT IS. THANKS."

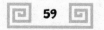

"What's it made out of? Bronze? Brass, maybe?" Phineus asked. Poseidon gave Zeus a worried glance, but Zeus gestured with his paws to be patient.

The whirring sputtered, and it took them a moment to recognize the new sound that replaced it: laughter. "MY SPEAR IS NO CHEAP TRINKET," Periphetes bellowed in his grating voice. "IT IS FORGED FROM MAGICAL ALLOYS!"

"Huh, no kiddin'?" Phineus sounded skeptical.

"YOU DARE QUESTION PERIPHETES?!" the voice bellowed. Periphetes lowered the spear so everyone could get a better view.

At that moment, Phineus grabbed the ribbon of Zeus's shield and yanked it upward, latching its tab onto the golden spear in Periphetes's hand.

"HEY!" Periphetes exclaimed.

"Now would be a good time to retract your doodad, Zeus," Phineus said.

Zeus hit the button on the side of his shield. *THIIIIPPPP!* The ribbon retracted, pulling the spear away from Periphetes. It landed with a clank between Zeus and Poseidon.

"You did it, Phineus!" Zeus picked up the spear and examined it. "You tricked Periphetes into giving up the spear!"

"See, lad?" Phineus brushed his paws together and then held them open. "No need to get your paws dirty."

"GIVE ME BACK MY PROPERTY!" Periphetes screeched. He stretched his metal arm but it wasn't nearly long enough to reach to the ground.

"Mind if I take a look, lad?" Phineus took the spear from Zeus, examining its shiny metal. "Ooh, nice and light." He called up to Periphetes. "You were right: magical alloys."

The metallic whine had become a constant grinding: Periphetes was bellowing with rage.

"I'm not sure you should be teasing that brute," Poseidon said.

Periphetes's eye flickered from red to green and then to a deep purple, his arm flailing more furiously than ever. The entire slab was shaking, wobbling, teetering. "I AM COMING FOR YOU, RODENTS!" Periphetes's voice grated.

"I'll find you on Mount Olympus, son," Phineus said. He pushed past Zeus surprisingly hard, knocking him into Poseidon's helmet. They both rolled backward just as the slab toppled to the ground, landing inches from their faces. *BRAAAAHHM!* The crash must have shaken all of Greece. The shrill whirring had stopped. Periphetes was silent.

Zeus stood up and dusted himself off as Poseidon righted himself in his helmet. The slab lay on its side, forming a massive metal wall that stretched in both directions. Phineus was nowhere in sight.

"I hope Phineus didn't get squished under that thing," Poseidon said.

"I ... I think I saw him jump clear," Zeus said. "At least I hope he did." Zeus turned around. "The spear! Poseidon, do you see the spear?"

Poseidon scanned the ground nearby but spotted only the aegis shield. "Last I saw it was in Phineus's paw."

The two gods glanced at each other. Zeus was about to

say something, when the slab began vibrating in front of them. The metallic whirring, faint and muffled, started and stopped, then started again.

Poseidon rolled away in alarm. "Perhaps Periphetes still has some fight in him."

"No point in waiting to find out," Zeus said, slinging the aegis on his forearm. "Let's go meet up with the others."

After searching one last time for the spear, Zeus and Poseidon headed back toward the Agora and their rendezvous with the other Olympians.

CHAPTER 8

OOD NEWS, OLYMPIANS," ZEUS announced when he and Poseidon arrived at the meeting place. "We found—oh, where is everybody?" Demeter was the only one there. She was leaning against one of the Agora's rope-wrapped pillars. "Athena? Ares?" Zeus called.

"They're not with you?" Demeter said.

"Why would they be with us?" Poseidon asked.

"I saw them both from Mount Olympus," Demeter explained. "They were rushing back from Crete toward uncharted territory."

"When was this?" asked Poseidon.

"About an hour ago. I yelled down to them, asked where they were going. Athena hollered that they were looking for you two. I asked why, but they didn't answer. They sure seemed to be in a hurry."

"Looking for us?" Zeus asked, glancing back the way they had come. "Why didn't they find us? We should've passed each other."

"You think they're in trouble?" Demeter sounded concerned.

"Athena can outsmart trouble," Poseidon said, "although Ares is usually the cause of it."

"It's not like Athena to not show up," Zeus said. "What if they had a run-in with the Minotaur?"

Poseidon shook his head. "It's a tad early to jump to the worst-case scenario."

"What do you suggest we do, then, sea lord?" Zeus said. "By all means, call the shots."

Poseidon looked across Greece to the big picture window and its red Mount Olympus Pet Center sign. Faint fingers of orange crept across the sky outside. "We could wait here for her and Ares to return, although who knows when that might be, and the hour grows late ... er, early."

"Artie and Callie will get here soon," Demeter added.

"Exactly," Poseidon agreed. "I suggest you two return to Mount Olympus and keep your eyes open for Athena and Ares. I'll do the same from the Aegean Sea."

"Works for me," Zeus said with a shrug.

The Olympians dispersed.

Zeus and Demeter scurried up to the palace on Mount Olympus. Zeus peered out across Greece. He watched Poseidon roll to the edge of the Aegean Sea, where his seahorses hauled their king up the cliff face by his lifeline until he was back in the ocean. The pufferfish opened his helmet's faceplate and swam into the open water, stretching his fins. He came to rest on his coral throne while a team of colorful shrimp cleaned his diving helmet.

Otherwise, not a creature stirred in Greece. Zeus had little to distract him from a growing sense of dread. He couldn't shake the feeling that Athena and Ares were lost in the maze, wilting in the heat, the latest victims of the Minotaur. Zeus's shoulders slumped.

"Nice digs!" came a voice from behind them.

Zeus and Demeter whirled to see Phineus leaning on his gnarled cane in the middle of the palace.

"Phineus!" Zeus shouted. "You didn't get smooshed!"

"Phineus?" Demeter was gobsmacked.

Zeus slapped his forehead. In all his concern over Athena and Ares, he'd forgotten to tell Demeter that they had found Phineus. "Phineus, meet Demeter. Demeter, Phineus."

"Ah, Demeter!" Phineus pointed with his cane. "I'm so happy to meet you!"

"Um, likewise," Demeter replied hesitantly.

"I'm starving, you see," Phineus said. "Be a good harvest goddess and conjure me up some grub, will you?"

Demeter stared at Zeus, unsure how to react. "Where'd he come from?"

"Poseidon and I stumbled upon him during our run-in with Periphetes," Zeus said.

"Pair-a-feeties?" Demeter repeated.

"He was a one-armed, spear-wielding slab monster," Phineus explained. "Don't worry. I dealt with him."

"Pretty neat trick the way you outsmarted that brute," Zeus said. "Of course, I would have walloped Periphetes if you hadn't come along."

"That was a lesson for you, son," Phineus replied. "You're the king of the gods—you should be using your brains, not your brawn." Phineus turned to examine the piece of cushion covered with shimmering fabric in the middle of Zeus's palace. "Ho-ho! The Golden Fleece! It works well here. Really ties the place together."

Demeter was hit with a sudden realization. "That's right: You helped Zeus find the Fleece! You can tell us how to defeat the Minotaur!"

Phineus waved a paw dismissively. "No need to bother yourselves with that bull-headed beast."

"Of course we need to bother with it," Zeus shot back. "He's taken our friends!"

"And he's slow-roasting everyone in Greece, in case you haven't noticed," added Demeter, fanning her face.

"This heat's good for the old bones." Phineus shook out his arms. "I'm telling you, Zeus, you have to stop being so paws-on, chasing down dragons and Minotaurs and such. That's what you have minions for." He waved at Demeter.

"Minions?" Demeter repeated coldly.

"I'm still waiting on that grub, harvest goddess." Phineus stared expectantly at Demeter. "Chop-chop."

Demeter crossed her four front legs and fumed.

"Help yourself to some Fuzzy Feast, Phineus," Zeus offered. He pointed to a bowl near the back of the Palace.

The old hamster hobbled to the bowl and started stuffing its little brown treats into his mouth, his back turned to them.

Demeter caught Zeus's attention. HE'S OBNOXIOUS, she mouthed.

"Huh?" Zeus said, not getting the message.

"What?" Phineus turned to face the Olympians, his beard full of crumbs.

"We were saying that Athena and Ares are in danger!" Demeter replied.

"Nonsense!" Phineus scoffed. "Are they Olympians or aren't they? They need to fight their own battles." He pointed his cane at Zeus. "You need to learn to delegate, lad. Do you know what 'delegate' means?"

"Uh, sure," Zeus said. "But maybe explain it anyway. For Demeter here."

Demeter stared daggers at Zeus.

"Delegate means to assign tasks to your underlings." Phineus had stopped cramming pellets of Fuzzy Feast into his mouth and was now stuffing them into his beard for safekeeping.

"In other words," Demeter said, "you think Zeus should boss everyone around."

"Of course! He's king. Bossing everyone around is literally his job. You should be helping him with this, Demeter." Phineus spread his arms and looked around the palace. "You two live in the lap of luxury up here. If I

were you, I'd never leave this place. Going on adventures and battling monsters ... that's for mortal heroes or your squad of little-league gods."

"Little-league gods?!" Demeter shot back.

Phineus coughed up a few crumbs. "I'd ask for a drink, but I can tell this is more of a serve-yourself kind of palace. Ah-ha!" He hobbled to the water bottle at the rear of the palace and started sipping noisily, oblivious to Demeter's withering glare.

"Good morning, Olympians!" came a voice from below. It was Artie, here at her usual time to begin her caretaking duties.

She was followed by Callie, who was lugging her big green tool bag. "Whew, the furnace is really working overtime this morning!"

Zeus and Demeter watched the humans from the pillars of the palace. "Artie's here and there's still no sign of Athena and Ares," Zeus said. "This is not good." He turned back to the water bottle to ask Phineus for advice.

But the soothsayer was gone.

CHAPTER 9

 EMETER HUNTED FOR PHINEUS AT THE REAR of the palace. "Where'd he go?"

"I … I don't know," Zeus said. "He just … disappeared. Like he did after he helped me find the Golden Fleece."

"So this is just a thing he does?" Demeter checked behind the aegis shield where Zeus had casually set it on the floor. "When he's not giving terrible soothsaying advice?"

"His advice isn't all terrible."

Demeter rounded on Zeus. "If it were up to Phineus, you'd just sit on your Fleece, pound Fuzzy Feast, and boss everyone around. That's so not you!"

"The word Phineus used was 'delegate,'" Zeus corrected

Demeter. "And maybe I don't need to dirty my paws with every little thing."

"This Minotaur isn't exactly a little thing, Zeus. Athena and Ares are missing. We're all about to melt in this heat. Greece needs you and your dirty paws now more than ever!"

"OH MY!" Callie exclaimed below.

"Now what?" Zeus grumbled, turning to see what was transpiring.

"Everything okay?" Artie said. She had been about to check the thermostat.

"My drill press," Callie said, standing over the toppled slab. "It's fallen over."

Both women knelt beside the defeated Periphetes. "How'd this happen?" Artie asked.

"No idea," Callie said. "I mean, it couldn't have been one of your critters. This thing is way too heavy. Help me turn it over so I can see if anything broke."

They muscled the slab onto its side. From his high vantage point, Zeus could see that Periphetes's eye was dark and lifeless. His armored arm hung limply as Callie inspected it.

"Huh," she said. "The drill bit's gone."

"Is that bad?" Artie asked.

"Nah. I got spares." Callie wrapped her arms around the end of the slab and slowly lifted it back onto its feet. She stepped on a rubber pedal at the slab's base. The machine whirred to life.

"Callie woke up Periphetes!" Zeus exclaimed, watching from Mount Olympus.

Callie immediately stepped on the pedal again and the machine went silent. (Zeus sighed with relief.) "It seems to be working okay," she said. "I need to get this thing next door so I can get started. You're still planning to come over and help me, right? I could really use an extra pair of hands today."

"Sure," Artie said. "Let me get everything squared away first." She went back to her morning routine as Callie dragged Periphetes through the portal to uncharted territory.

Up on Mount Olympus, Demeter turned to Zeus. "Sounds like Artie is leaving Greece early today! That'll give us the time we need to rescue Athena and Ares!"

Zeus was about to respond when they both heard the

strains of familiar harp music. Zeus and Demeter looked down to see Artie playing with her rectangular artifact.

"Welcome to Greeking Out," came the familiar voice of the Oracle from Artie's artifact, "your weekly podcast that delivers the goods on Greek gods—"

"We already heard this part," Artie said as her fingers danced across the shiny surface of the artifact. "Let's fast-forward to where we left off … here."

"Theseus resolved to rid the land of the Minotaur menace," the Oracle continued. "He delved into the maze beneath Crete."

"This is good timing," Demeter whispered. "Maybe we'll learn how to defeat the Minotaur."

"Theseus was brave and strong, but he wasn't a fool," the Oracle said. "He knew that if he entered the unsolvable maze, he might become trapped forever. Fortunately he had help from a friend: Princess Ariadne."

"Ariadne!" Demeter repeated. "We know her! The spider from the maze!"

"*Princess* Ariadne?" Zeus mused. "She didn't look like a princess."

"What's a princess supposed to look like, Zeus?" Demeter asked flatly.

"I dunno." The hamster shrugged. "Smaller fangs. Fewer legs."

"Since when is number of legs a qualification for anything?" Demeter waved her four front legs.

"Good point," Zeus said.

"Princess Ariadne was the daughter of the king of Crete," the Oracle was saying. "He was a mean ruler, known to send

innocent people into the maze to feed the Minotaur. But while her father was cruel and cowardly, Ariadne was kind and courageous. She saw in Theseus a hero who could defeat her father's monster. She offered Theseus a crucial tool: a spool of thread. 'Tie the end of this thread to the exit of the maze,' she told Theseus, 'and then you shall never lose your way.'"

"I'm starting to think that spider princess is worth finding again," Zeus said. "She probably has a lot of answers about the Minotaur."

Demeter was about to point out that she had suggested tracking down Ariadne the night before, but she bit her tongue. "Good idea. Ariadne would certainly know more on the subject than Phineus."

"Someone say my name?"

Zeus and Demeter turned to see Phineus slipping through the secret back door of Zeus's palace. He was slightly out of breath but surprisingly full of pep as he closed the gate behind him.

"Where'd you disappear to this time?" Zeus asked.

"Soothsayer business," Phineus said with a grin.

"I'll give you soothsayer business," Demeter muttered.

Zeus shushed them so he could hear the Oracle. "Now, Theseus entered the labyrinth with confidence. He had his wits, he had his fighting skills, he had Ariadne's thread to guide him out, and he had the legendary spear."

"The spear!" Zeus suddenly remembered. "Phineus, do you have the spear?! I lost track of it when Periphetes fell on us."

"What spear?" Demeter asked.

"Misplace your new toy already, lad?" Phineus said. He pointed his cane at the aegis shield and Hekate's torch, a relic that made magical light, lying nearby. "Don't you have enough doodads cluttering up the place?"

"You mind catching me up here, Zeus?" Demeter pleaded.

"We swiped a spear from Periphetes this morning," Zeus explained. "I'm pretty sure it's the weapon Theseus's dad hid for him. I was hoping we could use it to beat the Minotaur ... but I guess I kind of lost it."

"Easy come, easy go," said Phineus, reclining on the Fleece and popping a piece of Fuzzy Feast into his mouth. "I suppose you won't be tackling any Minotaurs today."

The Oracle continued. "Theseus stomped deeper into the

maze, the air growing hotter with each step." Then the familiar harp music began playing again. "And that's it for this week's episode of *Greeking Out*," the Oracle said cheerfully. "Theseus's daring mission will conclude next time. Will he slay the Minotaur? Will Ariadne's thread help him escape the maze? Tune in and find out." Artie's relic went silent.

"See," Phineus muttered, "even the Oracle doesn't seem to think this Minotaur mission is worth finishing."

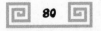

"Okay, Olympians," Artie said from below. She had been rushing through her morning routine, scooping Mutt Nuggets into food bowls and shaking fish food messily into the Aegean Sea. "I promised Callie I'd help her next door, so Mount Olympus Pet Center is closing early today." She locked the main portal to Greece. "I'll check on you all later—and I promise we'll get this furnace sorted out, too!" Artie walked through the portal to uncharted territory, leaving the Olympians unsupervised.

"Finally some peace and quiet." Phineus appeared like he was about to fall asleep on the Fleece.

Zeus sat silent for a long time. "What's the point of delegating if you don't have anyone to delegate to?" he finally said.

"Huh?" Phineus sat up.

"C'mon, Demeter," Zeus said. "Let's get Poseidon and head to Crete. We've got a date with a Minotaur."

Phineus stared in astonishment from the Fleece as Zeus stormed past him. "Are you seriously just going after the Minotaur empty-handed? No weapons? No preparation? No anything?"

Zeus paused to consider his relics, then slipped the

aegis shield on his forearm. "Not quite."

"Have you not heard a word of my soothsaying, lad?"

"The whole sooth and nothing but the sooth." Zeus opened the palace's back gate for Demeter and glanced back at Phineus. "Don't wait up for us, old-timer."

"What am I supposed to do?" Phineus asked, waving his arms at the palace.

"You know where to find the Fuzzy Feast if you get hungry." Demeter turned to Phineus and smirked. "This is more of a serve-yourself kind of palace, after all." She hopped through the gate after Zeus and let it fall shut behind her.

CHAPTER 10

"**K**IND OF RISKY GOING OUT WHILE ARTIE'S still here," Demeter said as Zeus paused at the top of the rope he used to climb down Mount Olympus.

"Yeah. I don't much care." Zeus peered toward the portal to uncharted territory.

"Well, all right, then." Demeter nodded. "I'll go get Poseidon. See you at the Agora." She leapt off the edge of Mount Olympus and glided to the Aegean Sea.

Zeus stepped off the summit and slipped down the rope to the foot of the Mount Olympus. He scurried to the Agora as fast as his feet would carry him in the heat. He was surprised to find Demeter and the lord of the oceans already waiting for him.

"Poseidon!" Zeus said. "Am I glad to see you! How'd you get here so fast?"

"Glad to see me?" Poseidon was wary. "Are you unwell?"

"Poseidon was already here waiting for us," Demeter said.

"I couldn't just twiddle my fins at home when Ares and Athena are missing and Greece roasts around me." Poseidon flourished his trident. "The Minotaur is most certainly to blame. The beast must be stopped."

"We're on the same page, sea lord," Zeus said.

"So what's the plan, Zeus?" Demeter asked as the trio began heading south along the Aegean Sea to Crete.

"It's a two-step plan, actually," Zeus said.

"Oh?" Poseidon was swimming fast to keep up in his dive helmet.

"Step one is to enter the maze on Crete," Zeus said. "Step two is to defeat the Minotaur."

Demeter stopped and exchanged a worried glance with Poseidon. "You think that's enough steps? I mean, as much as I hate to sound like Phineus, we are empty-handed."

"You met Phineus?!" Poseidon whirled to face Demeter.

"Met him. Don't like him."

"He didn't have the spear from that Periphetes brute?" Poseidon asked Zeus, checking him over as if hoping to see the spear tucked away in his chiton.

"No, unfortunately not. But we're not exactly empty-handed." Zeus brandished the aegis shield on his arm.

"You think you can defeat the Minotaur with just your grappling thingy?" Demeter asked.

"Hey, the aegis has gotten me out of some scrapes." Zeus angled the shield so its silver surface reflected the bright sunlight. "Don't forget we have Ariadne on our side, too."

"Ariadne?" Poseidon repeated. "The princess from the Oracle's tale?"

"That's her, sea lord," Zeus said. "She's the spider who helped us during our first run-in with the Minotaur. We can count on her."

"Are you certain of that?" Poseidon asked.

"Certainly I'm certain," Zeus said. "We're practically best friends."

"Then shouldn't finding her be part of this two-step plan of yours?" Poseidon asked.

"Fine," Zeus said. "Step one: Enter the maze. Step two:

Find Ariadne. Step three: Defeat the Minotaur. Everyone on board with that?"

"What a splendid plan!" came a high-pitched voice ahead of them. "It would be my honor to help you with it."

The Olympians were startled to see that a strange creature had materialized seemingly out of nowhere in their path. Its body, no bigger than Zeus's, sprouted dark brown fur. Leathery wings hung loosely at its side. In its clawed feet, the creature held the handle of a red rubber stick that ended in a scoop large enough for Zeus to sit in.

Zeus instinctively raised his shield to guard against the creature's razor-sharp talons. "Beware, Olympians. It's a Harpy!"

CHAPTER 11

POSEIDON AND DEMETER WERE LESS alarmed. Both had only the briefest brush with Harpies in the past, whereas Zeus once fended off an angry swarm, in the dark, with nothing but his torch and shield.

"This is one of those winged fiends that attacked you in uncharted territory, Zeus?" Demeter asked.

"Please don't include me in that colony of screeching cretins," the creature squeaked. "They represent the most wretched specimen of my kind, if you could even call them my kind. And good riddance to them, thanks to you."

"Are you certain that's a Harpy, Zeus?" Poseidon asked, looking the creature up and down. "I thought they were afraid of the light."

Holding his shield in front of him, Zeus approached the Harpy cautiously for a better view of its face. It wore what appeared to be a cloth band around its furry head, with holes cut out for its eyes. Zeus noted with surprise that its eyes were wide open—downright googly-eyed—despite the bright noonday sun filtering across the countryside.

"This can't be one of the Harpies that attacked me," Zeus said, lowering the aegis.

"How it warms my heart to hear you say that, Your Highness." The bat-like creature bowed low.

Zeus turned to the Olympians and jabbed a thumb at the Harpy. "I like this guy." He turned back and puffed up his chest. "No need to call me 'Your Highness,' friend. King Zeus will do. Or Zeus the Mighty. Either's cool."

Poseidon rolled his eyes.

"Yes, of course, King Zeus the Mighty." The Harpy practically squealed the name. "I should have known that's how you prefer to be addressed. I know so much about you. I know you're on a vital quest to defeat the Minotaur and end this atrocious heat wave. I know you would never fail us!"

"And you know that I don't know the meaning of the word fail," Zeus said matter-of-factly.

The Harpy swooned.

"What's your name, pal?" Zeus said. "I can't just call you Harpy."

"You may call me whatever pleases you, but my given name is Sinis, Your Highne—er, I mean King Zeus the Mighty. Apologies if I seem a little starstruck. I've heard tales of your legendary adventures since I was a pup."

"Well, you know," Zeus said, buffing a paw against his chest, "I try."

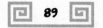

Behind Zeus, Poseidon scooched closer to Demeter and whispered, "This Sinis fellow is laying it on rather thick. I don't like it."

Demeter grunted in agreement and cleared her throat. "Excuse me, Sinis. You had mentioned something about helping us with our plan?"

"Yes, nothing would make me happier," Sinis said, then added quickly, "not that King Zeus the Mighty needs help from a humble Harpy. But perhaps I could … expedite your quest."

"Ex-pa-dite?" Zeus repeated the unfamiliar word. "You mean make things easier?"

"Yes!" Sinis clapped his wings. "Yes, exactly! You truly are as wise as you are courageous. Whoever said you shouldn't meet your heroes clearly never met you, King Zeus the Mighty!"

Demeter made a barfing motion at Poseidon. Something here felt wrong.

"I'm not as strong a fighter as you," Sinis went on, "but I am a strong flier, and I would be honored to shorten your journey." Sinis shifted his grip on the red rubber stick in his talons until the scoop at its tip rested on the ground before Zeus. "Climb aboard and I shall ferry you directly to the Minotaur, or even to your missing friends."

"You can take me to them?!" Zeus exclaimed.

"If that is your wish. Simply hop in." Sinis wiggled the scoop. "I'm afraid the seat isn't quite fit for a king, but it's more comfortable than the alternative." He flexed one of his razor-sharp claws.

"I'm sure it will be fine," Zeus said as he approached the scoop.

"Um, Zeus," Demeter interrupted. "Shouldn't we discuss this first?"

"What's to discuss?" Zeus said, stepping one foot aboard. "Sinis here is going to take me right to Athena and Ares!"

"Indeed I will," Sinis agreed, watching Zeus eagerly. "Unfortunately I can carry only one at a time, but I'll return for your allies here lickety-split."

"Zeus!" Poseidon's voice was filled with urgency. "Do not set another foot in that Harpy's conveyance! This offer is much too good to be true!"

"No more calling the shots for you today, fish lips," Zeus fired back. "It's clearly gone to your head." He lifted

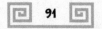

his other leg into the scoop-like seat and swiveled toward Sinis to settle in, stowing his aegis shield under his legs. "I see no harm in trusting our new flying fr-friend … ," Zeus sputtered out mid-sentence as he stared into Sinis's exceptionally huge eyes—never blinking, never even moving behind those eye holes in the cloth band around his head.

"Sinis, your eyes," Zeus muttered, panic rising in his chest. "They're … they're not right."

"You mean these eyes?!" Sinis shrieked, stooping close so that Zeus—and even Poseidon and Demeter nearby—saw the large eyes weren't really eyes at all. And the eye holes weren't really holes. It was all an illusion painted on Sinis's headband, which Zeus immediately realized hid the Harpy's real eyes from the blinding sunlight. "A Harpy doesn't need eyes to see, you flea-ridden fool!"

A series of rapid-fire clicks emanated from Sinis's head.

Zeus had a moment to wonder if these clicks helped the Harpy detect obstacles in the dark, but then he was buffeted by a gust of wind. Sinis had begun beating his leathery wings. They were airborne.

Zeus had been bamboozled. The Harpy carried the helpless hamster to a destination unknown.

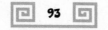

CHAPTER 12

EUS, JUMP!" HE HEARD DEMETER'S VOICE,
already alarmingly far away.

Without thinking, Zeus pushed himself up and
rolled over the side of the scoop-like seat. He grabbed the
scoop's lip with one paw and hung there, looking down,
shocked that Sinis had already carried him at least two feet
off the ground. Zeus immediately regretted leaving the
relative safety of the scoop.

But then a blur of motion below caught his eye. It was
Demeter leaping up at him in a powerful bound. She
reached him in a flash. "I got you, buddy!" she said,
latching on to Zeus's free paw with one of her front legs.

"You got me?" Zeus said, panicking as Sinis carried
them higher. "Who's got you?"

"Poseidon," Demeter said matter-of-factly. She pressed a slender hose into Zeus's paw. It was Poseidon's lifeline! The hose looped up from the sea lord's helmet to Zeus's paw, then snaked back toward the Aegean Sea.

"What do I do with this?" Zeus shook the hose, bewildered.

"Don't let it go, whatever happens," Demeter advised. "Poseidon is going to play tug-of-war with that turkey." She nodded up at the Harpy. "But he'll only win if you hold tight." Without another word, Demeter let go and glided back to earth.

Zeus now held the lip of Sinis's scoop in one paw and Poseidon's lifeline in the other, but he was still gaining altitude as Sinis flapped skyward. The Harpy was unaware that Zeus was tethered to the pufferfish far below.

Zeus could see Poseidon, who was no bigger than a marble at this altitude. He was swimming hard against his dive helmet, rolling it rapidly away from him and toward the Aegean. The pufferfish was pulling the slack from the lifeline. Zeus could see the hose was moments from going taut, at which point the tug-of-war would begin. Zeus braced himself, tightening his grip on both the lifeline and scoop.

VRRRRM! The jolt was so sudden and fierce that Zeus nearly dropped the lifeline, but Demeter's words—"don't let it go, whatever happens"—stuck in his brain. He held fast, caught between the lord of the sea and a fiend of the sky. Zeus's paws ached. They began to slip. He saw that the pufferfish was still rolling. He looked much larger now—much closer, along with everything else on the ground.

Poseidon was winning the tug-of-war!

"I'm … I'm being reeled in by a fish." Zeus giggled weakly. He was delirious from the heat and exhaustion, but he wasn't the only one worn out. Above him, Sinis had ceased his squeaky clicks and was now breathing in loud, ragged gasps, clawing at the hot air as he lost altitude.

"Let go of the scoop, Zeus!" came Demeter's voice from below, much closer this time. "Now!"

Again, Zeus acted without thinking. He released his grip and plummeted to the ground. It was a much shorter fall than he feared—just a few inches. Zeus flopped onto his back in time to see the scoop above him spring upward, released from the tension of Poseidon's lifeline. *THRUMM!* Like a catapult hurling a stone, the scoop launched a slender silver object into the air. Zeus

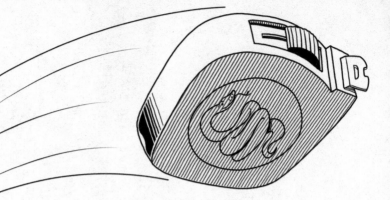

recognized it at once: his aegis shield. He followed its trajectory across the sky until it dwindled into a silver speck near the horizon, disappearing somewhere across the Aegean Sea to the east. Zeus's most cherished relic was gone.

A faint screeching pulled Zeus's attention to the northern horizon. Sinis had flown that direction, still clutching his rubber stick and screaming in frustration. A round shadow fell across Zeus. He sat up to see that Poseidon had rolled up to him, joined by Demeter.

"You okay, boss?" Demeter asked.

"We nearly lost you," Poseidon said.

"You were right about one thing, Poseidon," Zeus said, getting to his feet and dusting himself off. "That Harpy's offer was too good to be true."

CHAPTER 13

THE TRIO RESUMED THEIR JOURNEY TO
Crete in awkward silence. Zeus walked a few steps
ahead of Demeter and Poseidon, who wore a sour
expression. Demeter understood why: Zeus's ordeal with
the Harpy had cost them precious time and the aegis
shield. Now they really were empty-handed. To make
matters worse, Zeus hadn't even thanked Poseidon and
Demeter for plucking him from certain abduction.

Demeter considered speaking up to break the tension,
when Zeus turned back to face them. She held her breath,
not sure whether Zeus was about to make an awkward
situation worse.

"That Sinis guy turned out to be a real jerk, huh, gang?"
Zeus said. "It was great how you totally owned him in that

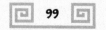

tug-of-war, Poseidon."

Demeter glanced at Poseidon and was relieved to see his expression softening.

"It was Demeter's idea to hand you my lifeline so I could tucker out your Harpy chum," Poseidon said.

"I knew Poseidon would overpower that blowhard," Demeter added.

"I had an advantage over the wretched creature," Poseidon said. "He had this heat to contend with. My water supply comes from the Aegean, so I'm always cool and comfortable."

"Good to know," Zeus said. "If it gets much hotter, I just might dive in there with you."

"Uh, no," Poseidon said. "I don't need any roommates, thank you."

"Fine, I didn't want to get my paws all pruny anyway." Zeus slapped a paw against Poseidon's helmet, then turned and continued on to Crete. The other Olympians followed, their spirits lifted.

Eventually, they reached the gap in the dunes that marked the entrance to Crete. Not quite an island, Crete was surrounded on three sides by towering dunes that held back the Aegean Sea. Each Olympian stepped through the gap warily, just in case the Minotaur had emerged from its maze below. Instead of the Minotaur, they found a wall of heat that made the rest of Greece feel like the Arctic.

"Is it just me, or is it, like, a million degrees hotter here?" Demeter asked.

"It's not just you," Zeus said, fanning his face with both paws. Nothing looked out of place from the previous morning. The farther they walked onto Crete, the hotter it got.

"I suspect all this heat is coming from the Minotaur's maze," Poseidon said.

"You suspect correct, Poseidon." Demeter was standing at the ledge of a rectangular pit near the far dunes of Crete.

Zeus joined her and held his paws over the pit. "Oh, yeah," he said, wriggling his fingers. "If I had a stick I could roast some Fuzzy Feast."

Poseidon rolled up next to them and peered into the pit. "Strange, I don't recall this hole being here when I called upon Crete in the past."

"It used to have a grate over it," Zeus said. "I bet that

Callie woman took it off. She's always messing with something."

"Or maybe the grate just melted from the—" A flash of red in the pit caught Demeter's eye. "Guys, it's her!"

The head of a massive spider wearing a ruby-encrusted tiara peeked out. She looked from Demeter to Zeus and to Poseidon, and then back to Zeus. "You, two-eyes, are you back here to defeat the heat?" Ariadne asked in her raspy voice.

"Yep, told you I'd be back," Zeus said confidently. "Oh, and call me Zeus, will ya? I mean, c'mon. I'm a king!"

"I know," Ariadne said curtly before disappearing back underground.

Zeus frowned. "Sheesh. Not much for pomp and circumstance, is she? I got more respect from that Harpy guy."

"I thought you said you two were best friends?" Poseidon asked.

"*Practically* best friends. *Practically*," Zeus clarified before quickly moving on. "Welp, steps one and two are done. Now on to step three." He dropped into the pit.

"Not sure this step will be as easy," Demeter said. She leapt down after Zeus.

"When is anything we do easy?" Poseidon took one last glance around Crete, then rolled into the pit, his dive helmet scraping and bumping as he dropped through the Minotaur's front door.

CHAPTER 14

OSEIDON LANDED WITH A THUD—
actually more of a clang. Water sloshed in his
helmet, clouding his vision. When the turbulence
settled, Poseidon could see the pit was actually the start of
a tunnel, its walls made of metal, leading into the gloom.
Afternoon sunlight streamed down from above, but the
tunnel itself glowed with a light of its own. A faint spark
of orange emanated from deep down the tunnel, its source
well out of sight.

Even Poseidon in his portable pool could feel that the
air was much hotter down here. Zeus and Demeter stood
slightly deeper in the tunnel. Zeus was fluffing out his
robes. Demeter's black antennae drooped around the gold
laurel wreath on her head. Both felt miserable. "Hot enough

for you?" Poseidon asked, trying to lighten the mood.

"Actually, yeah," Zeus replied. "You sure I can't just dip my feet in your helmet, Poseidon, old pal?"

"Yes," Poseidon said.

"I can?" Zeus said excitedly.

"I mean, yes, I am sure you can't," Poseidon said sternly. He noticed the spider watching him nearby. "Ariadne, I presume? Princess of Crete?" Poseidon tapped his trident against the three-pronged crown on his head as a salute.

Ariadne touched a fuzzy leg against her tiara in return.

"Why didn't you tell us you were a princess when we met in the Minotaur's lair?" Demeter asked.

"I figured it was obvious, harvest goddess." Ariadne regarded Demeter with her strange dark eyes, her fangs opening and closing.

Those fangs were exceptionally large, Demeter noted. She shuddered again, then said nervously, "So, uh, any tips on defeating this Minotaur monster?"

"One must tamp the coals to defeat the heat," Ariadne said.

"Right. Find the coals; give them a good tampin'," Zeus repeated, like it all made perfect sense. "Let's get going."

"The Minotaur isn't the only foe you'll face down here," Ariadne continued. "You'll need to master this warren first. The deeper you wander, the hotter it becomes. Lose your way and you shall succumb, never to see daylight again."

"So it's a good thing Zeus is here," Poseidon said.

"Thanks!" Zeus said at once, but then added, "Wait, why'd you say that?"

"It's well known that hamsters excel at solving mazes."

"Why does everyone think mazes are a hamster thing?" Zeus whined, his shoulders slumping. "The princess here can mark our path, right, Ariadne?"

"I would if I could," Ariadne said, "but I used up all my web thread leading you out yesterday." She wiggled her lower body as if that helped explain the situation.

"Wait, for real?" Zeus asked. "But I didn't bring any string. Did you, Demeter?"

"No," she replied.

"A long strip of lettuce?"

"No."

"You need none of those things," Ariadne interrupted.

"Then what do we do?" Zeus asked. "Follow my nose?"

"No," Poseidon said, "we follow my hose." The pufferfish waved a fin at the hose trailing behind him.

"The sea lord has come well prepared," Ariadne said. "You were wise to bring such a smart ally."

Poseidon fixed Zeus with a smug grin. "I guess my lifeline will come in handy for the second time today."

Zeus's cheek twitched. "Time's wasting," he said, stalking off into the gloom. Demeter and Poseidon fell in behind him, followed by Ariadne.

The group wandered deeper into the tunnel, their footsteps clanging softly against the metal floor.

Daylight faded quickly as they moved away from the entrance. Zeus wished he had Hekate's torch. "How do you see down here, Ariadne?"

"Have patience, two-eyes," Ariadne said. "Your vision will adjust in time."

Zeus was about to object when he noticed his eyes were in fact adjusting. But the growing heat was another story. There was no getting used to that. Zeus used his paws to fan his armpits.

The group reached a fork in the tunnel. "Which way?" Demeter asked. The orange glow seemed to emanate from both directions.

"I think I'll let our lifeline guy handle the navigation," Zeus said, moving aside so Poseidon could roll past. Something on the maze's metal wall caught Poseidon's eye as he stopped at the fork. He scooched close and examined the faint outlines of a cracked and grimy sign next to a seam that ran up both walls and across the ceiling and floor. "Demeter, would you mind cleaning that off?" He motioned to the sign. "I would but …" Poseidon waved his fins helplessly inside his helmet.

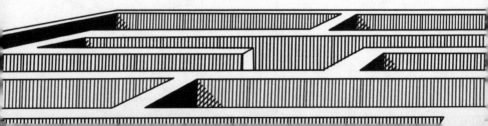

The grasshopper wiped at the sign until it revealed rows of strange characters:

Beneath the letters was an arrow pointing toward what looked like a ball of fire. The image seemed to indicate that the ball of fire was down the left fork.

"This way." Poseidon began rolling to the left, his lifeline trailing behind them all the way to the exit.

Zeus stared at the sign as he fell in step with everyone behind Poseidon. "Well, I could've figured that out."

And so it went for the next hour. Each time the Olympians reached a fork in the labyrinth, Poseidon

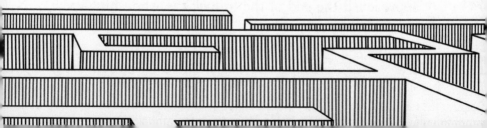

searched the wall for a sign and followed the direction of the arrow. The quest carried on.

Letting Poseidon call the shots was a new experience for Zeus—and he was surprisingly okay with it. If they ended up going around in circles, at least it would all be on the shoulders of the pufferfish. "Delegating," he muttered aloud. "Maybe Phineus is onto something."

"Surely we're nearly to the Minotaur," Poseidon said as he chose a direction at the next fork they came to.

Zeus saw Ariadne doing a strange dance, hopping from leg to leg.

"You okay, Ariadne?" Zeus asked. "You're moving like you've got ants in your pants."

"I have neither ants nor pants," she said. "Are you ready to defeat the Minotaur? I sense we are close."

"Sure," Zeus answered.

"Good," Poseidon called from ahead. "Because we're here."

They rushed in the direction of Poseidon's voice, which was nearly drowned out by a whooshing sound. As Zeus approached the end of the tunnel, the whooshing grew much louder. With it came a gale of broiling air. The floor felt scalding on his feet.

The Olympians and Ariadne clustered at the tunnel's end, all looking into a vast cavern. Zeus and Demeter knew this place. In the center stood a frightening yet familiar sight: a towering black beast with ash-smudged horns and nostrils of fiery orange.

The Minotaur.

"Okay, Zeus," Demeter said, standing behind the king of the gods. "We're ready for step three now."

CHAPTER 15

THE MINOTAUR REMAINED EVERY BIT AS terrifying as Zeus remembered. It loomed above the Olympians, its bull horns scraping the ceiling. The monster's beady eyes were lost in the gloom, mere embers compared to the fiery pits of its nostrils, linked by their chain. Beneath those nostrils was the Minotaur's mouth, its teeth clenched. The whooshing sound seemed to come from between the teeth, as if the Minotaur filled all of Greece with its hot breath. The teeth were still laced with strands of fur—much more fur than before, Zeus noticed with alarm.

The walls around the base of the cavern were riddled with passages similar to the one they'd just left—no doubt all leading to other metal tunnels in this maddening maze.

Zeus turned and was reassured to see Poseidon's lifeline trailing back the way they had come into the dimness of the tunnel. He was glad to have their escape route marked, at least.

The air in the cavern shimmered with heat. It wasn't like last time. This heat was crushing, exhausting. Zeus's vision doubled and tripled. His robes felt like they were about to catch fire. Demeter and Ariadne seemed to be wilting. Only Poseidon in his helmet seemed unaffected by the blistering heat.

"Okay, Ariadne!" Zeus yelled over the broiling gale. "We're here. Now what?"

"Now what *what*?" the spider asked, the rubies of her tiara glittering. Zeus noticed she was doing her funny dance again, hopping from leg to leg. He realized she was trying not to keep one foot on the hot ground for very long. "You came here to defeat this heat. Defeat it!"

Zeus's head was swimming. He glanced up at the Minotaur. It seemed to shimmy and sway, looming closer, about to smother him. Ariadne's cryptic tip replayed in his head: "Tamp the coals to defeat the heat." But what coals?

Zeus scanned the Minotaur's beady eyes, its mouth, its nostrils, and the chain that linked them. The nostrils!

"Bingo," Zeus croaked. "The coals are in the nostrils. That's his weakness. But how do I tamp them?" Zeus didn't have a single relic with him. If only he'd held on to Periphetes's spear!

He'd use his paws if need be. He had to try something. Zeus leaned into the searing gale and took a step forward, then another. The temperature seemed to leap ten degrees with every inch. The soles of his feet had become numb from the heat. And yet he pressed on. When he glanced up, expecting to be within striking distance of the Minotaur, it stood far away, another dozen steps at least. Zeus tried to take another step but couldn't. The heat was just too powerful.

"Hot enough for you?" shouted a voice nearby, making Zeus jump. Poseidon had rolled up next to him and was sitting calmly in his dive helmet.

"This is … no time to be funny … sea lord." Zeus could barely make himself heard over the blasting hot air. "This heat's a killer. I … I can barely move."

"It's getting to a low simmer in here, too, you know," Poseidon replied, wiping a fin across his forehead. "I bet I'd be sweating … if I could sweat."

"But you can still move," Zeus said.

"Certainly, I can still move." Poseidon rolled a few inches closer to the Minotaur to demonstrate. "But what can I do? Wave my trident menacingly?" Poseidon brandished his spear. The Minotaur didn't flinch. Instead, the hot wind seemed to step up a notch.

"I … I think that only made him mad," Zeus said. Exhausted, he fell to his knees, then rolled onto his side. The floor felt like embers through his robes. Zeus saw Demeter on her back at the tunnel entrance. Ariadne had her by a leg, pulling the grasshopper slowly into the relative cool of the tunnel's depths. "Good … good job, Ariadne," Zeus tried to yell. It came out as a whisper.

"Zeus, you need to figure this out. It's what you do, remember?" Poseidon said quietly to the overheated hamster.

"I … I can't take care of this one on my own, sea lord." Zeus barely had enough energy to talk, let alone fight the Minotaur. "This'll take teamwork. I … I really wish

Athena and Ares were here."

"Speaking of Athena and Ares, at least we know they didn't fall victim to the Minotaur," Poseidon said. "There's no way they'd fit through the maze to get down here."

Zeus propped himself on an elbow. "So where could they be?"

CHAPTER 16

ATHENA AND ARES CROUCHED AT THE entrance to a narrow valley in northern Greece. They were spying on a frail gray hamster who was rifling through a large crate deeper in the valley.

"Well, we sniffed him out," Ares whispered, panting hard in the heat. "That's the little guy who's been sending us all over Greece. Now what?"

"Now we lie low and see what he's up to," Athena answered.

"Why don't I just go ask him?" Ares stood and was about to stroll from their hiding spot when Athena pounced on his helmet, pressing it over his face.

"Will you sit tight?!" she hissed.

"Hey there!" the old hamster hollered.

Athena slunk low and grimaced, certain they'd been spotted. Beside her, Ares struggled to lift his helmet off his eyes with his front paws.

"Hey there!" the hamster repeated. "Sinis! How'd it go? Did you get Zeus all tucked in?"

"Zeus?" Athena whispered. A series of rapid-fire clicks pulled her attention back to the valley. She poked her head out from their hiding spot to sneak a peek. The old hamster hadn't spotted them after all. His attention was focused on a visitor descending from the sky on black leathery wings. It was a Harpy! The rapid-fire clicks sounded like they were coming from his head.

"I had him eating out of the palm of my hand," the Harpy said in a squeaky voice as he touched down beside the crate. The clicking had ceased. In his claws, the creature clutched the handle of a red rubber stick with a scoop on the end. "Zeus had climbed aboard my hopper and everything." The Harpy nodded toward the scoop at the end of his stick. "But then his friends sprung him loose."

"Sprung Zeus loose?" The hamster sounded disappointed.

"The sea lord used his hose as a leash," the Harpy explained. "I barely got away. It's hard enough flying in this heat solo, let alone with a passenger and a pufferfish weighing you down."

Athena struggled to make sense of what the old hamster and the Harpy were talking about. Next to her, Ares had finally got his helmet unstuck and was peeking into the valley. "Who's that bat guy?" he whispered.

"His name's Sinis, I think," Athena said curtly. "He's a Harpy."

"I thought Harpies couldn't see in the sunlight," Ares said. Both Olympians studied the large eyes poking through some sort of thin cloth mask on the Harpy's face.

"How could you let Zeus get away?!" The hamster was raging at Sinis. "You only had to fly him home and sidetrack him from his silly Minotaur mission. If I had just ten more minutes with the lad, I'm sure I could show him how to use his noggin instead of his paws. Now he's probably charging after the Minotaur with nothing *but* his paws!"

"Blame his buddies, not me." Sinis shrugged his wings.

Ares poked his head out farther for a better view of

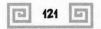

Sinis's talons. "Why's the Harpy got a ball chucker?" he asked Athena.

"What on earth's a ball chucker?"

"It's only the greatest thing in the world," Ares said enthusiastically. "Callie showed me one last week. She had me chasing balls all over Greece."

"Fascinating," Athena said, not really listening. She was focused on the old hamster and Sinis.

The hamster had gone back to digging in the crate. "I need you to take something to Zeus, Sinis."

"Sure, whatever you want," Sinis offered. "Throw it in the hopper."

"Here." The hamster held up what looked like a spear of golden metal and placed it carefully in the scoop at the end of Sinis's rubber stick. "I'd hidden this spear because I knew Zeus would be tempted to challenge the Minotaur with it, but now I imagine he's rushed headlong into that maze anyway. He doesn't stand a chance without it!"

"Then I'll make sure Zeus never gets his greedy little paws on it," Sinis said, beating his wings to take flight. "I hope the Minotaur pummels him!" Again came the series of rapid-fire clicks.

"Wait, what?" The old hamster's mouth dropped open.

"Wake up, old-timer," Sinis squeaked, gaining altitude with the spear in tow. "I didn't partner up with you so you could teach your pupil Zeus leadership lessons or whatever."

"Stop!" The old hamster made a pitiful leap for the spear in Sinis's scoop, but his paws barely brushed the smooth metal before it rose out of reach.

"I only played along so I could get revenge on the wretched rodent for having us Harpies kicked out of Greece!" Sinis beat his wings faster, carrying the spear away forever.

CHAPTER 17

"**W**HATEVER'S GOING ON HERE, WE HAVE to stop it!" Athena told Ares.

She leapt out from her hiding spot and pounced at the ascending Harpy, catching the edge of his scoop with a single claw on her paw. She easily could have brought Sinis crashing to the ground, but she didn't want to hurt him. Instead she simply clutched the scoop with her claw, keeping the Harpy from flying any higher, waiting for the him to exhaust himself.

"Not again," the Harpy squeaked, panting hard as Athena held him back. His clicks ceased.

The scoop, caught between Athena's claws and Sinis's iron grip, began bending lower and lower on its rubber stick, threatening to spill the spear to the ground.

The hamster scurried beneath the scoop and watched it eagerly, ready to catch the spear. "Good work, cat!" he cheered. "You nearly got it!"

Desperate to escape, the Harpy gave a powerful thrust of his wings and jerked the stick out of Athena's claws. *THRUMM!* The scoop sprung upward, launching the spear in one direction while Sinis flew off in another, screeching in fury.

Both Athena and the old hamster watched the spear sail across the sky, bound for a distant corner of Greece. "Ooh, ooh, I'll get it!" Ares barked. "I love this game!"

Before Athena could object, the god of war bolted out of the valley, slipping and scrambling, his helmet teetering wildly on his head.

"Athena!" the old hamster exclaimed once they were alone. "I'm so happy you found me!"

"Really?" Athena's tone dripped with sarcasm. "Ares and I only found you because we stopped playing your game."

"Game? What game?"

"The one where you've been sending us all over Greece to find Zeus and Demeter!" Athena said.

The hamster just stood and stared innocently.

"Oh, do you need a reminder? First you popped up on Crete and told us Zeus and Demeter were in trouble in uncharted territory. But when we got to uncharted territory, you sent us to the eastern shores of the Aegean. And when we got there, you sent us to the Northern Lands." Athena had been counting off each instance on a clawed paw. "All that running around made Ares miss lunch! Do you know how fussy he gets when he misses lunch?!"

The hamster tried not to wither beneath Athena's fury. "It might have seemed like I sent you on a wild-goose chase, but I had my reasons."

Athena ignored him. "We decided to stop playing your game and sniff you out. That's when we found you here up to who-knows-what with that Sinis character. Who is that Harpy, anyway?"

"Just an old acquaintance," the hamster said, "from my days in uncharted territory."

"What was that he said about you teaching Zeus lessons?"

"That's not important right now. Zeus and Demeter are in grave danger."

"Oh, really? That old line?" Athena scoffed. "We're not falling for that again!"

"For real this time." The hamster leaned against his cane, acting more frail than ever. "Zeus and Demeter are no doubt locked in a battle with the Minotaur as we speak. Surely you overheard me say as much to Sinis, before he tried to make off with my spear."

Athena couldn't argue with that point. Maybe this time he really was telling the truth. "Why's that spear so important anyway?" she asked.

"Periphetes's spear might be the only relic that can defeat the Minotaur," the hamster said. "I'm afraid Zeus is doomed without it. And we lost it."

"Found it!" Ares barked as he strolled into the valley carrying the spear in his mouth. He spat it on the ground in front of Athena and the old hamster. "Chuck it again! Chuck it again!" Ares said, turning in circles, his tail wagging furiously.

"The war god just saved the day," the hamster said, hefting the spear and shaking Ares's drool from it. "I'll tell you exactly where to go to save your friends. They'll need this." He handed Athena the shiny spear of golden metal.

CHAPTER 18

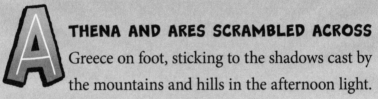**THENA AND ARES SCRAMBLED ACROSS**
Greece on foot, sticking to the shadows cast by
the mountains and hills in the afternoon light.
The two Olympians were on an urgent mission and dared
not risk getting caught by Artie or Callie, in case they
returned suddenly from uncharted territory.

"The place we need to go should be up ahead," Athena
said, pointing to the foothills beneath the lair of Kiko the
dragon in northern Greece.

"All tathe your wud fer it," Ares mumbled around the
spear in his mouth, spraying drool everywhere.

"We're here," Athena said, stopping beside a metal grate
in the north wall of Greece. Ares, whose Spartan helmet
had slipped down over his eyes, kept running until he

slammed into the wall with a clang. He sat down and began scratching behind his ear.

"Keep it down, war god," Athena said, looking toward uncharted territory.

"Oh-ay," Ares mumbled and jerked his helmet up so he could see again. He spat out the spear and Athena pulled it to her side. When he saw the metal grate in the wall right in front of him, Ares's eyes went wide. "They're in there?"

"That's what the old hamster said, but I can hardly see a thing through that grate. Give it a sniff."

Ares pressed his snout against the grate and snuffled for a few seconds. He sat down and stared at it, cocking his head.

"Well?" Athena asked. "What do you smell?"

Ares sniffed some more, then paused. "Grasshopper, hamster hair … old lettuce—but it all smells funny."

"Funny how?" Athena asked.

"You know when Artie heats up my treats for my birthday?" Ares said.

"Yeah…" Alarm started to creep into Athena's voice.

"It smells kinda like that. You know, extra crispy."

Athena sunk low on her paws—her gray fur poofed high in hackles—and bellowed into the grate. "Zeus! Demeter! Poseidon! Are you guys in there?"

Ares sat next to Athena and tilted an ear toward the grate.

"You hear anything?" she asked him.

He shook his head.

"ZEUS! DEMETER! POSEIDON!" Athena shouted again.

CHAPTER 19

EMETER! POSEIDON!" A FAINT, FAMILIAR
voice drifted down to the Minotaur's lair.

Zeus tried to push himself up to his knees
but failed. He desperately wanted to move closer to the
source of the voice, but he felt like a puddle on the floor.
Suddenly, he felt two fuzzy posts propping him up under
his shoulders. Wait, not posts. They were legs—Ariadne's
legs!

The princess was dragging him toward the tunnel
where they had entered. As he got farther from the
Minotaur, Zeus discovered he could get to his paws and
knees. The heat was no longer pinning him to the ground.
He patted the spider on her side as thanks, then crawled
toward the familiar voice. "Athena!" he croaked.

Zeus knew he wasn't loud enough. Just the effort of crawling had taken much out of him. Dizzy and weak, he was certain the Minotaur was about to snatch him from behind. With nothing to lose, he rolled onto his back and risked one more cry for help. "Ath—"

"ATHENA!" Poseidon yelled nearby. The pufferfish had rolled to a far wall and was yelling up at what looked like a cave entrance above him. "ATHENA!" he yelled again.

Back on the surface of Greece, Ares heard the distant cry. "It's Poseidon!" he barked at Athena. "Poseidon's down there! Hang on, buddy!" he yelled into the cave, then turned to Athena. "What do we do? We have to help them, but there ain't no way we're fittin' into that!" He motioned to the grate.

"We can't fit," Athena agreed, "but this can." She pushed the shiny spear into position with a paw. "Poseidon, heads up!" she yelled as she squeezed the relic through the slats of the grate.

Poseidon barely had time to heed Athena's warning before the golden spear fell from above. It glanced off his helmet and slid to a stop next to Zeus. The king of the gods recognized the relic at once. He closed his paw around it, then used it to lift himself off the hot floor. "Th-thanks, Athena!" Zeus yelled. "I can take it from here."

He turned to Poseidon and Demeter and Ariadne, who were all huddling in the tunnel entrance. "Time for step three," he said to them.

Now armed with the relic, Zeus stumbled back toward the Minotaur. Once again, it got hotter with each step. He turned back, defeated, and said, "I … I can't go any farther."

Ariadne replied, "You can't, but perhaps another can."

Zeus tried to figure out who Ariadne meant. He thought back to *Greeking Out*. The hero from the tale was Theseus, the mortal prince of Athens. But the only mortal down here was Ariadne. That's when he remembered. Theseus was the son of Poseidon, or so some believed. "Poseidon," Zeus muttered. "Of course. Poseidon!" he called weakly.

Poseidon rolled closer to Zeus.

"For the last time, can I take a dip in your helmet?"

The sea lord was about to protest but then saw this was no silly request. Zeus was on the verge of passing out from the heat. "Very well, Zeus. Just don't blame me when your paws get pruny." Poseidon positioned the helmet so its faceplate was up, then popped it open.

Mustering his last bit of strength, Zeus scrambled up the side of the helmet and hopped into the water. His feet found something squishy, which he stood on for support.

"Get off me!" It was Poseidon. Zeus was standing on the pufferfish's back.

"Ahhhhhh," Zeus said as he soaked in the helmet water up to his neck. He'd never felt such relief in his life. The water wasn't really cool—the heat of the Minotaur's breath had it at a low simmer—but it was certainly much cooler than the air outside.

Zeus was beginning to feel like his old heroic clearheaded self again. "Bet you never thought we'd be roommates!" he said to Poseidon.

"Roommates don't trod on each other! Step off!" Poseidon was starting to puff up, which was lifting Zeus out of the water.

"Calm down, sea lord!" The hamster hunched to keep the bulk of his body in the water. "Ow! Hey! Easy with that sea fork!"

"It's a trident!" Poseidon had poked Zeus's rump with it. "Just keep in mind you're in my realm now, so I'll be calling the shots!" Bubbles blew from Poseidon's mouth as he deflated. Zeus sighed in relief as he sunk deeper into the water.

"Now here's the plan," Poseidon said. "I'll scooch us to get you close enough to strike with Periphetes's spear. The rest is up to you. Deal?"

"Deal," Zeus said.

"Hold tight!" Poseidon pumped his fins and rammed the inside of his helmet, skidding it a few inches closer to the Minotaur. Bits of Zeus's fur drifted into Poseidon's mouth. "Blech! Must you get your wretched hair

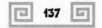

everywhere?" Poseidon rammed his helmet again with so much force it skidded nearly a foot. Water sloshed from the faceplate and dripped down the side of the helmet. It turned to steam the moment it hit the floor.

"Okay, we're just about there!" Zeus called. "Give me a second to get ready for the final charge!" Zeus steadied himself on Poseidon's back and began to stand up. "Hold still down there!" Zeus pulled his spear from the water and wielded it in front of him. The Minotaur stood just inches away.

The monster filled his world. All he could see were horns, or fiery nostrils, or teeth tangled in fur. Zeus aimed his spear. "Poseidon," he shouted, "charge!"

The sea lord didn't hesitate. He rammed into the side of his helmet with all the force he could muster. The helmet scooched one last time, straight into the side of the Minotaur. Zeus hoped his aim would be true.

He took a deep

breath and heaved the spear, burying its tip directly into the orange pit of the beast's nostril.

"Bingo!" Zeus yelled triumphantly.

He pulled on the spear, but it was stuck up the nose of the beast. Zeus tugged harder, putting all his weight behind it, but it didn't budge. "C'mon, gimme back my spear," he pleaded. His strength was fading fast now that he was out of the relative coolness of Poseidon's pool.

With his last ounce of power, Zeus twisted the spear—and suddenly the fire in the Minotaur's nostril extinguished. Zeus pulled, and this time the spear retracted easily. One nostril was out, but the cavern remained as hot as ever. Orange flames roiled in the other nostril. "One down, one to go," Zeus muttered.

Beneath Zeus, the Minotaur's teeth began to unclench, exposing the black pit of its mouth. The broiling gale increased, blowing bits of animal fur dislodged from the Minotaur's teeth. Poseidon had a front-row seat to this new horror. "Zeus, whatever you're doing up there, do it quick!"

Zeus barely heard Poseidon over the Minotaur's scream of rage. He aimed the tip of the spear at the other nostril, but it didn't reach. "Poseidon, these last coals aren't gonna tamp themselves. Can I get a boost?"

Poseidon puffed up. Zeus rose a couple of inches and wobbled, unsteady on the pufferfish's scaly back. He aimed his spear again but still couldn't quite reach. "A little higher!" Zeus yelled down.

"I'm ... I'm afraid I'm puffed to capacity," Poseidon said, still staring into the Minotaur's widening maw.

"I need you to get angry, sea lord!" Zeus cried. "If I don't get a boost, we're gonna be roommates forever!"

"Oh no we won't!" Poseidon suddenly puffed to nearly double his size, expanding to the limits of his helmet and sending Zeus clear out of it.

Zeus desperately reached for a handhold and grabbed the chain that hung between the nostrils. It seared his paw, but he refused to let go. He plunged the spear into the other nostril, twisted, and saw the fire extinguish. The spear fell to the ground with a clang and rolled beneath the Minotaur's stocky body.

Still dangling from the sizzling chain, Zeus watched

the Minotaur's teeth unclench completely. Its mouth went slack, dumping clumps of fur. Much of it fell into Poseidon's open helmet. "Yuck! Yuck! Yuck!" The pufferfish deflated to dodge the deluge of hair.

Hot and exhausted, Zeus let go of the chain and fell with a splash back into Poseidon's helmet. The sea lord gently pushed him to the surface so he could breathe.

Floating on his back surrounded by globs of soggy fur, Zeus stared upward and saw that the fire in the Minotaur had died completely. No longer did he feel that rush of hot wind on his face. The beast wheezed, then grew silent. It went dark, defeated.

Already the water felt cooler. "I … we did it," Zeus muttered to Poseidon.

"Yes, Zeus, we did it. Step three." Poseidon spit out a strand of hair. "Now would you mind vacating my abode? You are a dreadful roommate."

CHAPTER 20

ZEUS CRAWLED OUT OF POSEIDON'S helmet and slid down its side until his soaking feet hit the floor. It felt warm but no longer broiling. In fact, the entire room seemed cooler. Zeus shook off his damp fur. His enchanted robes, as usual, remained dry and spotless.

Beside him in the helmet, Poseidon was collecting clumps of floating fur with his trident and chucking them out of the open faceplate. "My minions will have their work cut out for them scrubbing this clean," he said, then knocked his trident against the wall of his helmet to get Zeus's attention. "Um, Zeus, would you mind?" He pointed at the open faceplate above him.

"Oh, of course," Zeus said. He slammed the faceplate

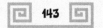

closed, then stood on his tippy toes and sealed its latches. "All buttoned up, sea lord." Behind them, the Minotaur sat dormant.

"That was amazing!" Demeter came running out to greet them. Her lettuce sash was brown and wilted, but otherwise she looked like her old healthy grasshopper self. "You guys beat the Minotaur!"

"You saw that?" Zeus asked.

"We saw it all from the tunnel," Ariadne said, joining the group. She waved two legs toward the entrance of the cavern, where Poseidon's lifeline still snaked out into the tunnel's dark mouth. "It was an inspiring feat of teamwork, courage, and ingenuity—and just in the nick of time."

"Well, you know," Zeus said, shaking water from his golden fur, "I try."

"Our gooses were literally nearly cooked," Demeter said. She raised a leg and high-fived Zeus, squishing water from his pruny paw, then slapped another leg against Poseidon's helmet more or less where his fin was. "Good thing you found that spear when you did. Where'd it come from, anyway?"

"It was a gift from the gods," Poseidon said.

"Which gods?" Demeter asked, confused.

"Us gods!" came the familiar voice from above. They all peered up to see Athena's blue eyes peeking through a rectangular grate far up the wall.

"Athena!" Zeus shouted. "You don't know how happy I was to hear your voice!"

"I'm here too, boss!" A wrinkled wet nose pressed against the grate. "Want me to fetch the spear again?"

Zeus glanced back at where the spear had rolled

underneath the Minotaur. "I don't think we're getting that back."

"Where've you guys been?" Demeter shouted up at them.

"More important, where are you now?" Poseidon asked.

"Northern Greece, under Kiko's lair," Athena said. "We have some serious catching up to do! Where can we meet up?"

"Crete!" Zeus shouted. "Find us on Crete!"

"Got it, boss!" Ares hollered. Athena's and Ares's faces disappeared from the grate. Zeus lifted Poseidon's lifeline. "Okay, gang. We're out of here. Follow the hose!" Zeus scampered toward the tunnel. Poseidon rolled along behind him.

Demeter hesitated when she saw that Ariadne wasn't joining them. "What're you waiting for, Ariadne? Don't you want to get out of here?"

"Get out of here?" She seemed mystified. "I live here. I'm a princess here."

"Come with us, Ariadne! You'll like it up there! You can live in the Bugcropolis with my buddies."

"The Bugcropolis." Ariadne pondered for a moment. "I know this place. I lived there once, as a spiderling. I don't think I'd be welcome there."

"What? Why?" Demeter asked.

"I'm a tarantula. Do you know what tarantulas eat?" Ariadne fixed Demeter with a cold stare.

"I … I don't imagine it's salad."

"It's not." Ariadne's fangs flexed.

Demeter shuddered. "Uh, okay, then. I'd love to stay and chat, but, uh, I should really get going and, you know,

I could use a bite to eat myself." She ran an arm over her wilted lettuce leaf. "Thanks again for your help with the Minotaur and, uh, don't be a stranger." She turned and hopped away after Poseidon.

Princess Ariadne, her kingdom of Crete now free from the heat, watched them go.

CHAPTER 21

THE MAZE'S PASSAGES WERE COOL BUT gloomy without the fiery glow of the Minotaur to light them. Zeus ran as fast as he dared in the dimness, careful not to let go of Poseidon's lifeline. Without it, the Olympians would have wandered in the maze for days ... or longer.

"Is it my imagination," Poseidon said as he rolled along behind, "or is it getting brighter in here?"

Before Zeus could answer, the Olympians turned a corner and saw a blinding light from far ahead: the exit. He could smell the Aegean Sea air. He climbed up Poseidon's lifeline out of the pit and into the sunlight. The next thing he knew, he felt the ground of Crete under his paws and a giant slobbery tongue slurping his face.

"You made it! You made it!" Ares barked at Zeus.

"Oh, yuck! Ares, stop!" Zeus flailed helplessly against Ares's licking assault. "Bad god!" Ares backed off.

"Am I glad to see you guys!" said Athena.

"I'd be glad to see anything at this point." Zeus's vision was starting to adjust to the afternoon light of Greece. He could see Ares pulling Poseidon from the pit by his lifeline and then giving the sea lord the welcome-home treatment.

"Oh, dear," Poseidon said as Ares slobbered all over his helmet. "I might as well toss this helmet into the abyss and get a new one."

"Cut Ares a little slack," Athena said. "We're just thrilled to see you all alive!"

"I could say the same thing about you," Zeus said, finally able to see clearly.

"We thought for sure you two had fallen victim to the Minotaur," Demeter added as she hopped up to join them.

"The Minotaur?" Ares plopped on his rump between the Olympians. "I wish we had run into the Minotaur. You guys are so lucky you got to play with him!"

"'Lucky' isn't the word I would use," Demeter said. "Where have you been?"

"We've been looking for you!" Athena replied.

"Looking for us?" Zeus said. "Why?"

"It's that old hamster's fault," Ares said.

"Uh, old hamster?" Zeus asked.

"Uh-oh." Demeter muttered.

"You met Phineus?" Poseidon asked.

"Yes," Athena said, "although now that you mention it, I don't think he ever told us his name. I just assumed he was Phineus. I remember Zeus once described him as a super-old hamster—"

"With terrible fashion sense," Ares continued. "That was this guy. He sent us scrambling all over the place. Kept telling us you were in danger, that we needed to rescue you."

"Why would I need to be rescued?" Zeus asked, as if the idea were preposterous.

The Olympians weren't quite sure how to answer. Athena interjected before the silence grew awkward. "I figured out Phineus was just leading us in circles," she said, "so we tracked him down."

"That's when things got real weird," Ares chimed in. "He was in cahoots with some Harpy."

"A Harpy?" Zeus and Demeter repeated, incredulous.

"Let me guess," Poseidon said. "The Harpy's name was Sinis?"

"Uh-huh, uh-huh!" Ares nodded so hard his helmet nearly fell off. "He carried around a ball chucker. He used it to make me fetch this spear he took from the hamster. It was fun!"

"Wait," Zeus said, "Phineus had Periphetes' spear?!"

"Someone talking about me?!" shouted the gray-haired hamster as he hobbled onto Crete. "Oh, do carry on with your little Olympian reunion. I just came here to see Zeus."

"Phineus?!" Zeus shouted. "What in blazes have you been up to?"

"Not too shabby, eh, lad? I guess I've still got it."

"Still got what?" Zeus was dumbfounded.

"The magic touch," the old hamster said matter-of-factly. "Why, I had your minions running all over Greece, doing my bidding. And I didn't have to lift a paw. That's how you rule."

"This was all some kind of game to you?!" Poseidon was outraged.

"Well, most of it," the hamster admitted. "The bit where Sinis turned on me wasn't part of the plan. He promised to help me teach you a lesson, Zeus. But it turns out Sinis and I had very different lessons in mind. Those Harpies can sure hold a grudge. You made a foe for life when you got his kind evicted from uncharted territory."

Before anyone could say another word, the portal to uncharted territory popped open far to the west. "Hello, Olympians! Miss me?" came a familiar voice. Artie, caretaker of Greece, had finally returned.

CHAPTER 22

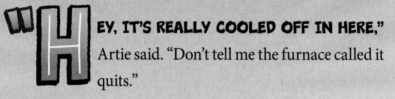

EY, IT'S REALLY COOLED OFF IN HERE," Artie said. "Don't tell me the furnace called it quits."

"Artie's back!" Ares barked.

"Hush!" Zeus clapped both paws across the pug's mouth, then immediately pulled them back and wiped slobber on his robes.

"Is that my favorite god of war?" Artie began walking in their direction.

"She can't catch us out and about!" Zeus shouted.

"Hide me!" the old hamster spoke up, panic in his voice. "Don't let Artie see me! We have a history, her and me!"

"Ares, where are you?" said Artie. She was rounding

the Aegean Sea. A few more steps and she'd be at the entrance to Crete.

"Oh, now you want our help?" Athena snapped.

"We're all in the same boat here, soothsayer," Poseidon said. "If she catches you, she catches all of us."

That gave Zeus an idea. "Ares, c'mere." He pulled the dog close and whispered into his ear. Ares's eyes widened, and then he nodded enthusiastically. He ran over to Phineus and bowed low.

"Hop on Ares," Zeus ordered the old hamster. "He can get you back to uncharted territory in no time. We'll stay here and distract Artie."

"That's using your head, lad!" the hamster said. He clambered clumsily onto Ares's back and grasped the spikes on the dog's collar for support. "Giddyup, war god! Take me home!"

"I'm taking you somewhere, but it ain't home!" Ares barked. He rushed out of Crete, making a beeline for Artie.

"Wrong way, you fool! Wrong way!" the old hamster shouted.

"Hey!" Artie yelled as Ares ran between her legs. "You think you're a greyhound all of a sudden? Get back here!"

155

The pug was running from landmark to landmark. "So here we have the Aegean Sea," he said to the old hamster clutching his collar. "And over here is the Agora."

"You take me to uncharted territory this instant, you fool, like Zeus commanded you to do!" the hamster shouted.

"That's not what Zeus told me to do at all," Ares said.

"How'd you like to see the Bugcropolis?"

Artie chased after Ares but couldn't get ahead of him. "What has gotten into you, war god?" she asked.

Back on Crete, the remaining Olympians huddled up. "What's Ares doing?" Athena asked.

"Taking that old-timer on a tour of Greece, just like he did to you two," Zeus said.

"Bravo, Zeus." Poseidon gave a little salute with his trident. "You managed to outmanipulate that manipulator!"

"You and Zeus sure sound chummy," Athena said, wonder in her voice. "I should prescribe adventures for you two more often!"

"What's that supposed to mean?" Zeus eyed Athena suspiciously.

"Why do you think I suggested you and Poseidon go hunt for Phineus together last night? You two were at each other's throats. You needed to bond!"

"Your plan worked like a charm, Athena," Demeter said. "Zeus and Poseidon were the ultimate team down in that cavern. They even managed to be roommates for, like, ninety seconds!"

"Eighty-nine seconds too long," Poseidon added, plucking a piece of Zeus's fur from his crown.

"Save the heroic stories for later," Zeus said. "Ares and Phineus are giving us the distraction we need to get home. Everyone scatter!"

Artie was too busy chasing Ares to notice the other Olympians. She reached down to grab the god of war as he bolted by—then snatched back her hand when she noticed something odd. "Ares, what in the world is on your back?"

CHAPTER 23

 NCE HE GOT HOME, ZEUS RAN TO THE pillars overlooking Greece just in time to see Artie recoiling from Ares.

"What's going on out here?" Callie had entered Greece from uncharted territory. "Hey, why's it so chilly?"

Artie was too distracted to answer. She made another grab for Ares as he darted by.

"Is Ares being a bad boy?" Callie asked.

"The human is talking to you, fool!" the old hamster yelled at Ares. "You're being a very bad boy!"

"Is that … is that a rat riding on Ares's back?" Callie exclaimed.

Up on Olympus, Demeter giggled as she joined Zeus at the pillars. "Phineus is definitely a rat."

"It's a rodent, but not a rat," Artie said. "I think I know which rodent it is, but I can barely believe it. I just wish Ares would settle down so I could get closer."

"He won't calm down for some Mutt Nuggets?"

Artie snapped her fingers. "Of course! Why didn't I think of that?" She reached into her pocket and pulled out some biscuit-like treats. "Ares, I have something for you!"

"Mutt Nuggets?!" Ares skidded to a halt, nearly bucking his passenger in the process. He darted back to Artie. "Gimme, gimme!" he barked.

"That's a good boy." Artie kneeled next to the pug and let him gobble treats from her palm. She scratched behind the war god's ear, then inspected the rodent who was wriggling beneath his spiked collar. "It's not a rat, Callie. It's a hamster."

"Wait, is that Zeus?" Callie said, stepping closer to examine Ares's passenger. "He is looking *rough*." She glanced over at Mount Olympus and saw Zeus staring back at her from his cage. "Nope … not Zeus."

Artie carefully pulled the gray hamster from Ares's collar and held him tight so he couldn't squirm away.

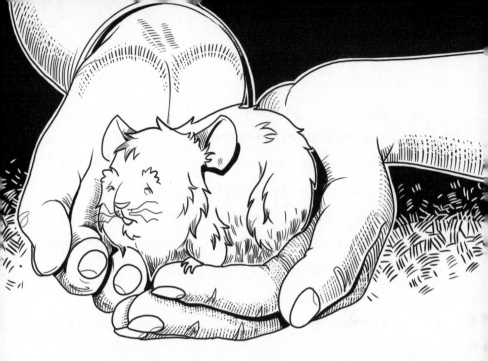

She tilted him to see his face in the light. "Not Zeus," she agreed. "This is Cronos!"

"Cronos?" Zeus repeated up on Mount Olympus. "No, no, his name is Phineus. Artie's got it all wrong. Sometimes she can be so dense!"

"Cronos?" Callie asked. "You know this little guy?"

"Yeah," Artie said, turning the hamster over in her palm as she inspected him. "He's older and grayer, but this is definitely Cronos. He's one of my original rescues, part of the group I called the Titans. Bit of a stinker, to be honest. Always getting out of his cage and bothering the other animals. But he disappeared ages ago."

"So how'd he get back here?"

Artie rubbed the old hamster under the chin, which made him squirm even more. "I have no idea." She stood and carried Cronos to Mount Olympus.

Demeter leapt out of sight before Artie could slide open the front gate to the palace. Artie reached in and dropped the gray hamster on the piece of Golden Fleece.

"Cronos, meet Zeus."

"Oh, we've met," Zeus muttered, glaring at Cronos.

CHAPTER 24

THE OLD HAMSTER STARED BACK AT ZEUS defiantly. Neither spoke. Demeter had a million burning questions but was afraid to break the awkward silence. Finally, she couldn't stay quiet any longer. "You're not a soothsayer, are you, Phineus?"

Her question spurred Zeus to speak up. "You're not even Phineus, are you, Phineus?"

"Well, in my defense," the gray hamster said, "I never said I was Phineus."

"Oh, that's such a load of hamster pellets!" Zeus exclaimed. "You've been posing as Phineus the soothsayer ever since I found you in uncharted territory."

"Actually," said the old hamster, holding his paws up, "it was you who said I was Phineus the soothsayer. I just

never corrected you."

"But—but ..." Zeus thought a moment. He had assumed the old hamster was Phineus, the blind soothsayer from the Oracle's tale of the Golden Fleece. "Okay, but why all the soothsaying, then? All your help with the Fleece?"

"You call it soothsaying, Zeus," Cronos said. "I call it guidance, from one king to another." He climbed off the piece of Fleece and walked to the nearby bowl of Fuzzy Feast, where he reached in and helped himself to a particularly juicy morsel.

Demeter scoffed. "When were you a king?"

"A long time before you two showed up," Cronos said around a mouthful of crumbs. "When I ruled the Titans, there was none of this business of leading them on adventures. I talked them into doing everything for me. I *delegated*." He grabbed another nugget of Fuzzy Feast.

"Well, your delegating didn't work this time," Demeter said. "Athena and Ares figured out your game. They got the spear from you and then came and helped us. And in the end we all defeated the Minotaur together."

"But can you imagine doing all that without ever having to leave Mount Olympus?" Phineus said to Zeus, spreading his arms wide.

"Where's the fun in that?" Zeus asked.

A sudden commotion out in Greece caught their attention. Zeus and Demeter turned to see Callie holding a massive gray rectangle with one hand while banging it with the other. Clouds of dust and clumps of hair dropped from the rectangle with each impact.

"Gross," Artie said as closed down the cash register for the night. "What's that?"

"This," Callie said, holding up the rectangle, "is why your furnace was working overtime. You need to change the filter more often. It was so clogged with pet hair that it popped right out of its compartment. Shut the whole system down until I put in a new filter."

"Oh, shoot, okay, I'll keep that in mind," Artie said.

She zipped up her coat while Callie swept up her mess. The two crossed Greece to its main portal, where Artie switched off the lights.

"See you tomorrow, Olympians," Callie said.

"Stay out of trouble," said Artie.

The two stepped out into the night and locked the portal behind them.

Zeus turned away from the pillars. "As I was saying, Cronos—"

But Cronos was gone.

"You've got to be kidding me." Demeter peered around.

A series of rapid-fire clicks outside grabbed Zeus and Demeter's attention. They looked through the pillars to see Sinis the Harpy flying across Greece on his leathery

wings. In his talons he held the rubber stick with the scoop—what Ares called a ball chucker. Sitting in the scoop was Cronos. The old hamster waved his gnarled cane in farewell.

"So that's how Phineus—er, Cronos got around so fast," Demeter realized. "He was getting rides from that Harpy."

"Yeah, those two seem made for each other." Zeus shook his head as he watched hamster and Harpy soar away into the evening gloom. "Something tells me we haven't seen the last of them."

CHAPTER 25

"PHINEUS WAS REALLY CRONOS?" ARES asked for the third time as he ran behind the *Argo*.

"So it would seem," Zeus said from his spot at the bow of the vessel. Poseidon and Demeter stood on the deck nearby while Athena steered from the helm. Zeus had been catching everyone up on his talk with Cronos on Mount Olympus. Ares, as usual, had a hard time grasping the finer points of the conversation.

"He had you fooled this whole time?" Poseidon twirled his trident. "You must be dreadfully embarrassed."

"He never told me he wasn't Phineus," Zeus said defensively. "I thought he was giving me soothsaying advice. How was I supposed to know he was trying to manipulate me into being something I'm not?"

"You didn't take anything Cronos/Phineus said seriously, did you?" Demeter asked. "About delegating and stuff?"

The other Olympians watched Zeus carefully.

"Of course not!" Zeus replied.

"Good," Ares said. "I don't like any kind of gating. I go where I want!"

"Olympians, we're here," Athena said, putting a stop to the conversation. The *Argo* had arrived in Crete. Athena steered toward the far dunes—and the entrance to the Minotaur's maze. She brought the *Argo* to a halt with a slap of the big control button at her feet. *BOOP!* The whir of the *Argo*'s motor faded, leaving the Olympians in silence.

Zeus hopped down and walked to the pit entrance. Heat welled up from it, although it wasn't nearly as intense as it had been earlier.

"Hmm," Demeter said, joining Zeus at the pit, "does this heat mean the Minotaur's stirring again?"

"If so, he's not nearly as strong as before." Zeus held his paws over the pit. "This feels pretty manageable."

"Actually, this feels pretty nice." Athena had plopped down and was stretching her legs over the heat rising from the maze entrance.

"Yeth, thith ith nithe." Ares's tongue was flapping in the warm breeze coming from the pit.

"Perhaps having a Minotaur living under Greece isn't such a dreadful thing after all," Poseidon said.

"Only if we can make sure the beast behaves," Demeter added.

"And that nobody winds up lost in his maze," said Zeus.

"Leave that to me, two-eyes," came a raspy voice from below.

Ares leapt back while Athena hopped to her feet and arched her spine, hackles rising. Both were shocked to see a massive spider watching them from inside the pit.

"Stand down, you two," Zeus said to Athena and Ares. "This is Princess Ariadne. She's on our side."

"Spiders get that big?!" Ares asked, the tiniest bit of fear creeping into his voice.

"Ares!" Poseidon exclaimed. "Don't tell me you're actually afraid of something."

"I'm not afraid of nothin'," he said, backing away until

his stocky rump collided with the *Argo*.

"Why do your friends fear me?" Ariadne asked, the rubies on her tiara sparkling.

"You got me," said Demeter. "If anyone should be afraid of you, it's me. And yet I'd follow you anywhere, Ariadne."

"Ariadne saved us from the Minotaur," Zeus explained to Athena and Ares. "She's the only reason we made it out of the maze."

"Twice," Ariadne said.

"Right, twice," Zeus agreed.

"Is it true the Minotaur stirs again?" Poseidon asked the spider.

"Yes, but he seems more even-tempered this time," Ariadne said.

"So we don't need to go wallop him?" Ares asked.

"For the time being," Ariadne said, "no. The Minotaur's fiery heart warms Greece. This would be a cold land without him."

"Awww," Ares whined. "I guess I'll never get to play with the Minotaur."

"What do you suggest we do, Ariadne?" Zeus said.

"Warn everyone in your realm to stay out of mine," she said. "I'll keep an eye on the Minotaur."

"Keep all six eyes on him, will ya?" Zeus said.

No longer afraid of Ariadne, Athena sat down beside the pit and stretched her legs over it once again. "Ahhhhh," she purred, soaking up the warmth. "This is much better than battling a Minotaur." She seemed on the verge of falling asleep.

"Ahem? Athena!" Zeus said. "You still with us?"

"Oh, all right." The cat got up reluctantly.

Zeus peered down into the pit at Ariadne. "You'll tell us if anything changes with the Minotaur, right?"

"You'll be the first to know, two-eyes," she replied. And then her glittering tiara faded out of sight.

"Okay," Demeter said. "What's next?"

"Let's go find out," Zeus said. "All aboard the *Argo*."

Everyone scrambled back onto the vessel while Ares chased his tail impatiently. "Where to, Zeus?" Athena asked.

"I think I'll leave that up to Poseidon."

The pufferfish whirled on Zeus, his eyes wide in surprise. "You really mean that, Zeus?"

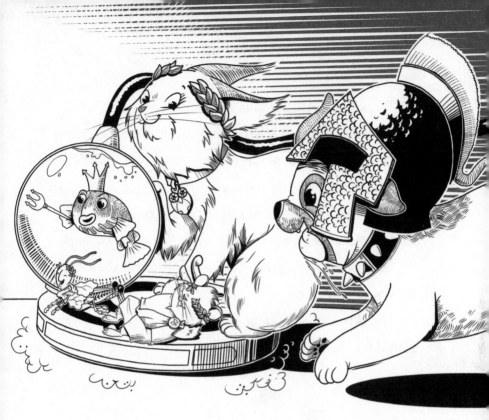

"Why not? You've been doing an okay job calling the shots so far."

"Yeah, Poseidon," Demeter agreed, "you're a natural at this!"

"Okay, okay." Zeus held up his paws. "Let's not get carried away here. This is only a temporary thing so I can take a breather." He reclined on the deck and crossed his paws behind his head. "It's exhausting work being the king of the gods."

"Very well," Athena said to Poseidon. "Where to?"

Poseidon twirled his trident as he pondered their destination. "Athena, get us out of Crete. Chop-chop!" he ordered sternly.

"Oh gods, I created a monster," Zeus groaned, tugging his golden laurel crown over his eyes.

"Aye, aye, sea captain!" Athena answered as she kicked the vessel into gear.

The *Argo* rolled off of Crete. The Olympians were bound for their next adventure.

THE TRUTH BEHIND THE FICTION

Land of Gods and Monsters

Ancient Greece was both a time and a place: a civilization that flourished near the Aegean and Mediterranean Seas around 2,500 years ago. It was a realm of heroic mortals ruled by fearsome gods who didn't always get along. Or so Greek mythology would have us believe. How seriously should we take these myths? Are they history lessons or fairy tales? Actually, they're a bit of both.

What Is a Myth?

A myth is a special kind of story, often recited orally, that tries to explain something. Myths helped people make sense of their world in the days before science and internet search engines. Why does the sun set? Why does the earth shake? Where did the world come from? Myths offered supernatural solutions to these mysteries by explaining that a gaggle of gods and goddesses controlled them. These mythical stories inspired the ancient Greeks to build temples and hold lavish events to appease the gods. The original Olympic Games were actually created in honor of Zeus.

Olympian gods had their own colossal temples. This one was built for Zeus in Athens and once had more than a hundred columns.

The Myth Makers

No one knows who first came up with the Greek myths. Most were sung around fires as songs or recited aloud until about 750 B.C., when a poet named Homer composed his two epic poems, *The Iliad* and *The Odyssey*. Performed by bards in villages around Greece, these stories were an account of a conflict called the Trojan War and featured Greek gods and mortal humans. Homer didn't bother explaining who his characters were because ancient Greeks already knew all about them.

To Be Continued ...

Even after the civilization of ancient Greece fell under Roman rule more than 2,000 years ago, Greek culture lived on and its myths were not forgotten. The Romans simply adapted them for their own use. Modern-day authors, playwrights, and screenwriters do the same thing, tweaking and retelling myths for audiences.

Today, Greek mythology's influence can be found everywhere from movies to store names and clothing brands. The Greeks' myths established the "hero's journey"—a formula featured in stories ranging from Star Wars to Harry Potter: a hero yearning for adventure, a series of dangerous trials, help or hindrance from the supernatural, and victory over impossible odds. Sound familiar?

Athena marches in the middle of a parade of gods on this ancient Greek vase.

The ancient Greeks worshipped 12 major gods known as the Olympians (because they gathered on Mount Olympus, the highest peak in Greece). These gods were all-powerful, and yet in some ways they were relatable, possessing the same emotions—love, sadness, anger, jealousy—as everyday mortals.

Zeus

King of the gods, the big cheese of the deities, Olympian numero uno, Zeus ruled from Mount Olympus and held domain over the heavens and the land beneath them. He brought order, making sure the sun rose every day and none of his fellow gods got out of line. No Olympian dared challenge him—at least not to his face.

Poseidon

God of all bodies of water—from the mightiest ocean to the piddliest puddle—Poseidon commanded the tides, raised tsunamis, and calmed tropical storms using his enchanted trident. Sailors in ancient Greece prayed to Poseidon for safe passage. In mythology, he was a brother to Zeus, and, like some siblings, they didn't always get along.

Athena

Goddess of wisdom, Athena was the brains of the Olympian operation, having outwitted Poseidon and even Zeus at various times. She also inspired creativity. When ancient Greeks were struck with a brilliant idea, they thanked Athena. When they wanted to build something—from a wagon to a ship—they prayed to her for inspiration.

Ares

Few Greek gods were as feared as Ares, the god of war. He was a brute, a force of chaos. He attacked first and asked questions later. Warriors screamed his name before charging into battle, hoping he would grant them courage.

Demeter

As the goddess of food and harvests, Demeter was beloved by ancient Greeks. One bad season of crops could lead to disaster. Demeter kept everyone's belly full, so people worshipped her as a symbol of prosperity and abundance.

Artemis

A guardian and caretaker, and a crack shot with her bow, Artemis was the goddess of animals. In particular she protected young and helpless animals until they could take care of themselves. Artemis lived in the wilderness, tending to her furry and feathered friends.

AMAZING ARTIFACTS

Greek mythology is rich with relics enchanted with astounding powers.

The Aegis

Forged in the workshop of Hephaestus, god of blacksmiths, the aegis was portrayed as an indestructible shield or armor fashioned from gold, with a texture like snakeskin. Both Zeus and Athena wield the aegis in various myths.

Theseus's Spear

Prince Theseus, the hero of the Minotaur myth, didn't face the bull-headed beast unarmed. He wielded a spear that his father, the king of Athens, had once hidden beneath a stone slab in the countryside as a test of his son's worthiness to rule.

The Myth of Theseus and the Minotaur

From *Greeking Out*, we learned of a fearsome monster that lurked beneath the island of Crete. It was the Minotaur, a creature with the body of a human and the head of a bull. It waited at the heart of a maze for unsuspecting victims who lost their way. The last thing these poor souls felt was the Minotaur's hot breath. Only one hero, Prince Theseus, was courageous and strong enough to defeat this terror—but he didn't do it alone.

Athens's Avenger

Prince Theseus's father was the king of Athens, and Theseus became its protector. He was inspired by the exploits of Heracles, the famous hero. He wanted to become just as well known. Young Theseus rid the land of a series of villains, including Periphetes and Sinis (turn the page to read more about them). In no time at all,

Theseus grew up in a small city south of Athens, unaware that his father was Athens's king. He only found out after he discovered a pair of sandals and a weapon hidden beneath a slab in the countryside. The king had hidden these items knowing only his son would find them.

Theseus became Athens' favorite hero. But his greatest challenge was yet to come, and it wouldn't happen in Athens.

The Monster in the Maze

Minos, the king of Crete, was cruel and petty, everything Theseus was not. Beneath his island, King Minos built a maze, also known as a labyrinth, to contain a nightmarish monster, the Minotaur. The king kept his beast well fed with people taken from city-states that Crete had defeated in war, including Athens. Every nine years, Athens had to send fourteen tributes, seven boys and seven girls, to feed the monster in the maze. Prince Theseus couldn't stand seeing innocent Athenians sent to their doom. He decided to defeat the Minotaur.

The maze beneath Crete was constructed by Daedalus, a brilliant craftsman and inventor. He later built wings from feathers and wax so he and his son Icarus could escape Crete's mad king. Icarus perished in the attempt when he flew too close to the sun.

Thread of Hope

Theseus took the place of one of the fourteen kids and entered the maze beneath Crete. He was confident he could defeat the Minotaur, but the labyrinth was another concern. Theseus rightly feared he might get lost within its confusing corridors and wander forever. Fortunately, Princess Ariadne, the daughter of King Minos, was not cruel like her father. She wanted the Minotaur gone as much as Theseus. So she gave him a spool of thread and instructed him to tie one end to the entrance of the maze so he could find his way out.

Unwinding the coil of thread as he went, Theseus led the tributes deep into the maze, assuring them that he could protect them. The air grew hotter from the Minotaur's breath, until Theseus finally found the beast at the maze's heart. Fighting with swiftness and cunning, he cut the Minotaur down. Ariadne's thread led the way to the exit and safety. Theseus and the tributes emerged from the maze victorious. The Minotaur would never threaten anyone again.

Bad Company:
The Villains of the Minotaur Myth

For every heroic mortal in Greek mythology—every Theseus and Jason and Heracles—there was an army of crooks and cutthroats, bullies and bloodthirsty beasts. Here are the troublemakers who inhabit our tale ...

Periphetes

The roads outside Athens were once a dangerous place, prowled by thieves. The worst among them was Periphetes. According to some myths, he was a Cyclops, an ancient one-eyed creature with superhuman strength. Not all Cyclopes were mean-tempered—some possessed great blacksmithing skills and forged magical weapons for the gods. But Periphetes was good at only one thing. He would ambush travelers

and pound them with his bronze club, then swipe their belongings. His robbing spree ended the day he met Theseus. Periphetes brandished his shiny club, threatening the hero. Intending to outwit him, Theseus complimented Periphetes on his fine weapon and asked if he might test its weight. Periphetes obliged, and Theseus turned Periphetes's own weapon against him.

Sinis

To terrified residents of the Athenian countryside, he was known as the "pine-bender": a bully who pulled the tops of pine trees to the ground and used them to catapult victims high into the air. The bully's name was Sinis. Few who encountered him lived to tell the tale. Theseus, however, used Sinis's own evil tactics against him. He bound the thief in the boughs of his pine tree and launched him on a one-way trip out of Athens.

Harpies

With human bodies, batlike wings, and bottomless appetites, Harpies were monstrosities sent by the gods to torment Phineus the soothsayer in the myth of "Jason and the Argonauts." Soothsayers were important people in ancient Greece because they could predict events, but Phineas was so good at foretelling the future that the gods blinded him out of jealousy, and then dispatched Harpies to devour his food before he could eat a morsel, which is why Phineus called them "Snatchers."

Cronos

Before Zeus and Demeter, Athena and Ares, and all the other Olympian gods, there were the Titans—the original deities of Greek mythology. Cronos, king of the Titans, was courageous, but cruel. He ruled out of fear and jealousy that his own children might someday rise up against him. That day eventually came when his own son, Zeus, joined the other Olympians and clashed with the Titans over control of land, sea, and sky. Just as Cronos had feared, Zeus and the Olympians won. They divided the regions among themselves and cast Cronos out, bringing an end to his reign.

Athens, Georgia, is about 5,600 miles (9,000 km) away from Athens, Greece.

SERBIA

KOSOVO

NORTH MACEDONIA

ALBANIA

ITALY

TYRRHENIAN SEA

ADRIATIC SEA

IONIAN SEA

Mount Olympus ◆

GREECE

Delphi •

Corinth •

Mycenae •

Sparta •

Strait of Messina

SICILY

Mount Olympus was the highest peak in ancient Greece. The Greeks believed it was Zeus's home, where he held court over the Olympians.

At the height of its power around 500 B.C., ancient Greece was a sprawling empire. Its geography divided it into many separate regions, but they all shared the same language, culture, and—most important—mythology.

Theseus's hometown of Athens was one of ancient Greece's most bustling cities and a center of Greek culture. It was named for the goddess Athena, whom the Athenians worshipped in a colossal temple known as the Parthenon.

MED

MAP KEY

◆ Ancient location
● Ancient city
▮ Area controlled by Greece around 500 B.C.
— Present-day boundary

BULGARIA

To Colchis →

BLACK SEA

T U R K E Y

Sea of Marmara

Troy

AEGEAN SEA

Thebes

Athens

Miletus

Crete was the largest of hundreds of islands in ancient Greece. King Minos ordered the construction of a maze beneath the island to hold the fearsome Minotaur.

Sea of Crete

C R E T E

Before Theseus defeated the Minotaur, he rid the countryside around Athens of bandits and bullies, including Periphetes and Sinis.

Knossos

ITERRANEAN SEA

0 ———— 100 miles

0 ———— 100 kilometers

BOOK 3:
The Labors of Hairy-Clees

"**K**EEP YOUR EYES OPEN, OLYMPIANS,**"** warned Zeus the Mighty as he crouched on the shore of the Aegean Sea. "The Hydra's close."

The Olympians huddled around their kneeling leader.

"Really?" Demeter the grasshopper peered about nervously, her eyes wide. The pillars of the Agora, meeting place of the Olympians, stood to the west. The coast of the Aegean Sea stretched from the north to the south. In the distance stood the rugged hills of Greece, crammed with their colorful relics and crates of goodies. Demeter saw no sign of a five-headed swamp monster. "What makes you think the Hydra's here?"

"This." Zeus dipped a finger into a puddle near his knee. When he lifted it, slime trailed off his fingernail. "We're hot on its trail."

"That's … gross." Demeter scrunched up her face.

Ares the pug pushed his head past Demeter and sniffed the puddle, his wrinkly nose poking through the cheek guards of his Spartan war helmet. "I recommend you don't drink that," he offered helpfully.

"Um, thanks," Demeter replied sarcastically. "I'll try to resist."

"No problem," Ares said with a goofy grin. "Happy to help."

"Let's keep moving!" hollered a pufferfish bobbing just offshore in the Aegean. "We have the Hydra in our grasp!" Before the Olympians could answer, the fish sped off to the north, his three-pronged crown cutting a wake like a shark's fin.

"You heard the sea lord. Poseidon's in charge today." Zeus stood up and tried to find something to wipe his slimy finger on. He reached out to clean it on Ares's fur, but the pug took off after the pufferfish.

"'Poseidon's in charge today,'" Athena repeated, shaking her head. The golden owl charm on her collar jingled. "Those are four words I never thought would come out of your mouth."

"What can I say?" Zeus shrugged. "We Olympians have had serious mojo lately. I like it." He reached out to wipe his finger on Demeter's back.

"Gotta go!" The grasshopper bounded out of reach.

"Mojo?" Athena repeated as she watched Demeter fall into step behind Ares. "You mean, like, we're not constantly arguing?"

"Right, we're getting along and doing our thing. You know, mojo!" Zeus lifted his finger slowly—then jabbed it toward Athena to wipe on her fur.

"Nope," Athena said as she leapt away from Zeus, twisted in midair, and landed at a trot behind Demeter, Ares, and Poseidon.

Zeus sighed and shook his finger to clean it as best he could, then hustled to follow the other Olympians north.

"It's thataway," Poseidon hissed in a low voice. He pointed east along the shoreline with his trident.

Zeus and the Olympians craned their necks to see.

"You sure that's the Hydra?" Zeus squinted. "I don't see five heads."

"I don't see *any* heads," added Athena.

"Sure I'm sure," Poseidon said. "That creature has been camping on the shores of my realm every night for at least a week."

"Camping?" Athena repeated. "You mean it's just sleeping there?"

"That doesn't sound so bad," Ares said.

"You don't know these sea monsters like I do," Poseidon replied. "Today it's camping. Tomorrow it will be throwing a beach party with Scylla and Charybdis and the sirens. Next we'll be dealing with an entire sea-monster theme park."

"And … that would be bad?" Ares asked, tilting his head.

"Yes, it would most certainly be bad," Poseidon answered firmly. "We need to convince the Hydra to leave while it's still on the beach. There'll be no getting rid of it once it slips into the water."

"So that's why you organized this hunting expedition!" Zeus exclaimed. "The Hydra is about to become your

problem, and you want help while it's still everyone's problem."

Poseidon puffed up in protest, but Zeus raised his paws. "Relax, sea lord," Zeus said. "I agree, we should handle the Hydra together. We've been on a real winning streak lately."

"It's true. We found the Golden Fleece, and we defeated the Minotaur," Demeter said, counting off their achievements.

"Point is, we're a well-oiled machine—thanks to my amazing leadership skills." Zeus waited for the Olympians to confirm. They stared back blankly, so he moved on. "No reason to dial it back now." He began walking east toward the Hydra's hunched form. "Everyone take your places."

CHAPTER 2

AKE UP, SLEEPYHEADS!" ZEUS THE Mighty bellowed up at the five-headed monster snoozing on the shore of the Aegean Sea. "Nappy time's over!"

The Hydra didn't stir. Its heads hung limply at the end of long, scaly necks that sprouted from a stocky chest. Slimy drool dribbled from three of its five mouths into a puddle that reeked of low tide. A titanic helmet of iron bars encased the Hydra's heads in a sort of protective cage. Even hunched in sleep, the beast towered over Zeus, despite the hamster's best efforts to stand tall and puff out his chest beneath the fabric of his chiton.

Zeus noticed the ground was littered with crumbs of Mutt Nuggets, Ares's favorite snack. He picked up a morsel. "I said, wake up!" He chucked it at the Hydra.

It was a good throw. The Mutt Nugget struck the Hydra square in the chest, hitting what appeared to be a small crystal. The crystal lit up, and the Hydra swiveled slowly in Zeus's direction. It had awakened!

The five heads began whirling around its body, just short of scraping the inside of its strange iron helmet. The heads spun slowly at first, then faster and faster.

A breeze rippled the laurel-wreath crown on Zeus's head. "That's right—rise and shine!" he yelled.

The Hydra hissed, spitting mist. Its five necks kept whirling around and around within the helmet, kicking up a gale that blew a slobbery fog over Zeus.

"More like 'rise and slime,'" Zeus muttered as he wrinkled his nose and pushed damp fur from his eyes. His royal robes, as always, lay neat and dry. "Okay, we can either do this the easy way or the hard way!"

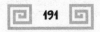

Acknowledgments

Like any Greek myth, the creation of *Zeus the Mighty* was its own odyssey. Becky Baines at National Geographic Kids dreamed up the idea of Mount Olympus Pet Center and invited me to embark on this quest. Nat Geo's Kate Hale led the charge and never let the adventure drag. Catherine Frank—oracle of children's literature, pug devotee—found the most exciting narrative path for us to follow.

Illustrator Andy Elkerton continues to bring our Olympian heroes (and their foes) to vivid life, while design director Amanda Larsen creates the cool look for each book. Production editor Molly Reid makes sure I write right while ensuring the world of Mount Olympus Pet Center is portrayed consistently from the first page to the last. Photo director Lori Epstein lends her expert eye.

Dr. Diane Harris Cline, a professor of history and classics at George Washington University and an expert on all things Greek, is my beacon for staying within sight of the source material. She's written the book on ancient Greece. Literally. It's called *The Greeks: An Illustrated History* and was as valuable to me in this process as any of Zeus's relics.

Finally, my wife, Ramah, is an endless source of inspiration and patience. She keeps me from getting lost.

—*Crispin Boyer*

All illustrations by Andy Elkerton unless otherwise noted below:
176, Pamela Loreto Perez/Shutterstock; 177 (UP), kanvag/Shutterstock; 177 (LO), Rogers Fund, 1906/Metropolitan Museum of Art; 178 (UP), DeAgostini/Getty Images; 178 (CTR), Luisa Ricciarini/Leemage/Universal Images Group/Getty Images; 178 (LO), Harris Brisbane Dick Fund, 1950/Metropolitan Museum of Art; 179 (UP LE), PRISMA ARCHIVO/Alamy Stock Photo; 179 (UP CTR), adam eastland/Alamy Stock Photo; 179 (UP RT), The Cesnola Collection, Purchased by subscription, 1874-76/Metropolitan Museum of Art; 179 (LO LE), Heritage Image Partnership Ltd/Alamy Stock Photo; 179 (LO RT), Bequest of John L. Cadwalader, 1914/Metropolitan Museum of Art; 180, Edward Burne-Jones - Tile Design - Theseus and the Minotaur in the Labyrinth/Darling Archive/Alamy Stock Photo; 180-181, Andrey Kuzmin/Shutterstock; 182, Roman mosaic, early 4th century AD; Villa Romana del Casale, Piazza Armerina, Sicily, Italy/Bridgeman Images; 183 (UP), bronze statue of harpy, 1st Century; Aosta, Museo Archeologico Regionale; De Agostini Picture Library/A. de Gregorio/Bridgeman Images; 183 (LO), Statue of Cronos, Knights hall, Royal castle, Warsaw's Old Town (UNESCO World Heritage List, 1980, Poland), De Agostini Picture Library/G. Sosio/Bridgeman Images